The Energy of Success:
How to Turn Dreams into Reality

Turn Off Your Inner Critic and You
Will Achieve Your Boldest Goals

Ronald Pits

The Energy of Success:
How to Turn Dreams into Reality

When I started my journey to success, my dreams seemed unattainable. I often asked myself: how can I turn what seems impossible into reality? In my book "The Energy of Success," I share what helped me transform dreams into real achievements. This book is not just a collection of theoretical ideas, but a practical roadmap that has been tested in real life. I have gathered all my insights and methods that allowed me to overcome internal barriers and doubts, and now I am ready to share them with you.

Here's what you can expect from the pages in this book:

- Step-by-Step Guides – I have detailed how to set goals and create a plan to achieve them, so you can easily apply this in your life.
- Methods for Overcoming Barriers – Practical tips that helped me deal with doubts and fears that hinder progress.
- Success Stories – Personal examples and inspiring stories of people who proved that the impossible is possible.
- Tools and Resources – Recommendations for using tools that made the process more organized and efficient.
- Interactive Exercises – Activities that will help you reinforce what you've learned and apply it in real life.

"The Energy of Success" is your personal guide to overcoming obstacles and realizing your boldest plans. If you are ready for change and want to learn how to turn dreams into reality, this book is for you. It's time to take the first step towards success — let's begin together!

Dedicated to my beloved dad!

Table of Contents

Chapter 1: Breaking the Chains of Dreams
How to free yourself from your limiting beliefs and start believing in your ambitions. In this chapter, we explore how to overcome internal barriers that prevent you from believing in your dreams and how to change your mindset to achieve great goals.

Chapter 2: The Magic of Goals
Learn why clearly formulated goals are not just words but the key to your success. Learn how goal-setting can become your guide and how to use them as a powerful tool for achieving success.

Chapter 3: Creating the Dream
How to visualize your dreams so they become your action plan. Learn how to create clear and inspiring visions of the future that will help you move in the right direction.

Chapter 4: Mapping Your Path
A step-by-step guide to creating a roadmap that will lead you to success. Discover the secrets of building an effective action plan that will turn your dreams into reality.

Chapter 5: The Power of Habits
How to build daily habits that bring you closer to your goals. Explore how small, consistent actions can significantly speed up your journey to success.

Chapter 6: Overcoming Fear
Methods and strategies for combating the fear of failure and self-doubt. Learn how to overcome internal barriers and confidently pursue your goals.

Chapter 7: The Magnet of Motivation
How to maintain high levels of motivation despite obstacles and challenges. Discover ways to sustain energy and motivation throughout your journey.

Chapter 8: Masters of Time
How to manage your time effectively and discover different ways to prioritize your time to ensure maximum productivity. Learn how to manage your time so that every action brings you closer to success.

Chapter 9: Secrets of Successful People
Examining the habits and strategies of people who have already achieved what you're striving for. Get inspired by the examples of successful individuals and adopt their best practices.

Chapter 10: Transforming Failures
How to learn from failures and use them for personal growth and goal achievement. Discover how setbacks can become a powerful source of strength and growth.

Chapter 11: The Power of Support
How your environment and support network can become your catalyst for success. Explore the importance of support and how to choose the right people who will help you on your path to success.

Chapter 12: Plan B: When Things Go Wrong
Strategies for adapting and adjusting plans in the face of changes and uncertainties. Be prepared for unexpected turns and learn how to become flexible with your plans.

Chapter 13: Time-Outs for Reflection
Why it's essential to pause and assess your progress and strategies. Learn the practice of regular self-evaluation, which will help you adjust your course and move toward success.

Chapter 14: Actions and Reactions
How to act proactively and use your actions to create opportunities. Discover the secrets of a proactive approach and learn how your actions can create new opportunities.

Chapter 15: The Magic of Small Things
How small steps and details can be impactful on achieving big goals. Learn how attention to detail can significantly influence your success.

Chapter 16: Tools for Success
An overview of useful tools and technologies that will help you on your path to success. Familiarize yourself with tools that will make your journey more effective and organized.

Chapter 17: Secrets of Personal Effectiveness
How to develop personal effectiveness and manage energy for better results. Learn how to become more effective and productive in your efforts.

Chapter 18: The Power of Affirmation
How to celebrate your successes and use them as motivation for new achievements. Learn to celebrate your victories and use them as a source of inspiration for future accomplishments.

Chapter 19: Long-Term Perspective: How to Think Ahead
Planning for the future. Learn how to think in the long term and develop strategies that prepare you for your future success.

Chapter 20: The Art of Networking How to Build and Develop Meaningful Connections for Success
In this chapter, we will discuss the importance of networking, how to find like-minded individuals, and how to effectively communicate with those who can assist you on your journey toward achieving your goals.

Chapter 21: The Psychology of Success How Your Mindset and Attitude Influence Achievements
We will explore various psychological aspects that contribute to success, including positive thinking, self-confidence, and emotional management, and learn how to apply these concepts in our lives.

Chapter 22: Conclusion: How the Energy of Success Turns Dreams into Reality
Final thoughts; integrating all aspects on the path to achieving your dreams. Final advice for reaching success.

Chapter 1:
Breaking the Chains of Dreams Introduction: Breaking Barriers

Dear Readers, In this chapter,
I will share how I overcame internal barriers and freed myself from limiting beliefs that once held me back from believing in my dreams. The path I took was full of challenges, doubts, and failures, but it was this journey that taught me how to change my mindset and achieve great goals. I will share my personal experiences to inspire you to overcome your own barriers and believe in your ambitions.

Part 1: The Shadows of Psychological Limitations

When I began my journey to success, I faced many psychological barriers. Born into a low-income family in one of the U.S. states, I was surrounded by limited resources and biased opinions, that people like me could never truly achieve their dreams.

I remember how, as a child, I dreamed of becoming a designer. Many told me it was impractical and that I had no chance of success. Those words were like heavy chains binding my ambitions and slowing my progress. Self-confidence, as it turned out, was my biggest obstacle. These internal doubts and fears were like a weight I carried without even realizing how much they were holding me back.

The Road to Success as a Designer

I recall drawing beautiful illustrations and dreaming of becoming a designer. I enrolled in art school and worked on my skills every day. But often, thoughts crept in: "This isn't for you. You'll never achieve big success." These thoughts were fueled by those who considered my passion a waste of time. Despite this, I kept working hard, even though internal doubts sometimes overshadowed my belief in my own abilities. It all began when my father noticed my drawing skills and encouraged me to study design. He provided real-life examples of how the design profession could be rewarding. At the same time, my fifth-grade art teacher, who led our class, noticed how enthusiastically I drew during every lesson. One day after class, she approached me and said, "You have a real talent. I want you to try to get into art school." I felt a spark ignite inside me. It was both exciting and frightening, but her belief in me inspired me.

From that day on, my journey into the world of art began. The teacher worked with me for an entire year, preparing me for admission. She opened the doors to an art studio where I spent every day after school. This place became my second home. I remember how, at the beginning of my studies, I would enter the studio with a slight sense of awe. The walls were covered in student paintings, each reflecting the individuality of its creator. I had never seen anything like it.

Every morning, I eagerly made my way to the studio. Together with my teacher, we explored the theoretical foundations: composition, color and anatomy. I learned not only how to draw, but also how to see the world differently. She showed me how to convey emotions on canvas, and every time I finished a piece, I awaited her reaction as if it were the most important exhibition.

In the evenings, when I returned home, I shared my progress with my father. He always listened with interest and he supported and encouraged me. He would bring me new materials: paints, brushes and sketchbooks. He wasn't an artist himself, but he always said, "If you want it, you will succeed." His support gave me confidence, and I felt like I could overcome any obstacles that were in my way.

I began spending more time in the studio than ever. My friends and I organized group sessions, discussed ideas, and shared our impressions. I remember how we worked on projects together, spending hours experimenting with different techniques. That time became not only an education for me but also a true celebration of creativity.

All this time, my teacher believed in me. She organized exhibitions for us, and I saw for the first time how my works brought joy to viewers. It was an incredible feeling — standing among my paintings, knowing they could touch someone. Each exhibition gave me new strength, and I realized that this was not just a hobby, but a calling.

When the day came for admission to art school, I was full of excitement and hope. I knew that I had people behind me who believed in me, and that gave me strength. I had done everything I could, and when it was time to wait for the results, I felt that everything I had experienced that year had led me to this important milestone. My dream was closer than ever, and I was ready to move forward without looking back. After a whole year of dedicated study in the art studio, I had finally reached the moment I had dreamed of — admission to art school. Each day spent at the easel was filled not only with hard work but also with inspiration. I devoted myself to drawing with full dedication, learning new techniques, working on compositions, and experimenting with colors.

Part 2: Breaking Free from Limiting Beliefs

Overcoming limiting beliefs began with the realization that many of these thoughts were temporary barriers, and not intrinsic parts of me. I began to understand that fears and doubts often stem from our internal dialogue, and recognizing this was my first step toward freedom. At first, I started analyzing my thoughts. Every time a negative belief surfaced, I asked myself, "Where did this thought come from? Does it have any real basis?" More often than not, I found that these thoughts were rooted in past failures or the opinions of others that had no relevance to my current reality. I learned to distinguish between constructive criticism, which helps me grow, and destructive doubt, which only drags me down.

This process of self-awareness became a form of cleansing. I began writing down my thoughts and emotions and reflecting on them. This helped me see which beliefs were truly helpful and which were merely hindrances. I realized that all negative mindsets could be challenged and redefined. For example, whenever I thought, "I can't do this," - I would replace it with, "I can learn and improve."

With each new revelation, I felt my limitations receding. I stopped seeing myself as a victim of circumstance and started viewing myself as the active creator of my own life. I set goals and worked toward them, recognizing that every failure was just another step on the road to success.

This process taught me to accept my weaknesses and work on them rather than hide them. I became more open to new opportunities and challenges, understanding that I had the right to make mistakes and be imperfect. Ultimately, I realized that the deepest limitations exist only in my mind, and overcoming them meant embracing the freedom to be myself.

I began developing a more sustainable business model that included diversifying income streams and more meticulous financial management. With the understanding that startups require flexibility, I decided to venture into trading as an additional pursuit. This idea came to me after I noticed a demand for specific products in the market. I started researching which products were in demand and how best to sell them; it was a new but exciting path.

I started small, using my previous knowledge in marketing and advertising to promote the products. At first, these were small orders, but over time, through persistence and a strategic approach, my business began to grow. I learned not only how to sell but also how to build relationships with customers, which turned out to be the key for successful trading.

This experience not only helped me regain confidence in my abilities, but also showed me that every misstep is an opportunity for learning and growth. I continued to evolve as an entrepreneur, using knowledge from the past to create something new and successful. While pursuing trading, I remained connected to the world of creativity, allowing me to blend my passions with business.

In this way, I not only recovered from the agency's collapse but I also discovered new horizons. I learned to draw lessons from my mistakes and use them as a platform for further growth. Now, I felt more confident and prepared, ready to face new challenges and build a successful future.

Part 3: Shifting Mindset and Setting Goals

To change my mindset and start believing in my dreams, I applied several key strategies:

Positive Affirmations: I started each day with positive affirmations that reinforced my belief in my abilities. For example, I would repeat to myself: "I am capable of achieving great things. My efforts will lead to success."

Positive affirmations for success:
- "I am capable of achieving any goal I set for myself."
- "Every day, I become more successful and confident."
- "My efforts and hard work lead to outstanding results."
- "I attract success and prosperity into my life."
- "My dreams and ambitions come to fruition thanks to my determina-tion and hard work."
- "I am worthy of all the good life has to offer."
- "I possess unlimited potential for success."
- "Every failure is an opportunity to learn and improve."
- "I control my destiny and create my own success."
- "My success inspires and motivates others."
- "I attract positive and supportive people into my life."
- "My confidence grows stronger every day."

- "I can overcome any obstacle on the path to my goals."
- "I can use my unique talents and abilities to achieve success."
- "My ideas and actions lead me to great achievements."
- "I believe in my abilities and will allow my potential to fully unfold."
- "I am tuned for success and joyfully welcome it."
- "I am capable of overcoming any difficulties and learning from them."
- "My success is the result of my persistence and positive thinking."
- "Every day, I take a step toward my dreams and strive for new heights."

How to Use Affirmations: A Practical Guide
Affirmations are positive statements that can help change negative thoughts and strengthen your self-confidence. Here are a few steps on how to effectively use affirmations in your life:

- **Identify goals:** Start by defining what you want to change or achieve. This could be increased confidence, better health, or career success.
- **Create affirmations:** Write short and positive statements that align with your goals. Formulate them in the present tense, as if they've already happened. For example:
- "I am confident in my abilities."
- "I attract success."
- "I accept myself as I am."
- **Repeat affirmations:** Set aside time each day to repeat your affirmations, either in the morning or evening. Repetition will help solidify new beliefs.
- **Use visualization:** While repeating affirmations, visualize how your life is improving. Imagine achieving your goals.
- **Write them down:** Keep an affirmation journal where you write down your statements. This helps track progress and provides extra motivation.
- **Be consistent:** Practice affirmations regularly. The more often you repeat them, the stronger their impact on your mindset.
- **Surround yourself with positivity:** Use sticky notes or reminders in visible places like your mirror or desk to keep your affirmations in mind.
- **Listen to audio:** Create or find recordings of affirmations that you can listen to during walks or relaxation.
- **Practice patience:** Remember that change takes time. Give yourself space to see results.
- **Update affirmations:** As you grow and change, adjust your affirmations to keep them relevant. Affirmations are a powerful tool for personal growth. Allow them to become part of your daily routine, and you'll see how your life starts to change for the better.

Visualizing Success: I often imagined myself achieving my goals, and this process of visualization became an important part of my life. Every time I thought about my dreams, I would close my eyes and immerse myself in the images that inspired me.

I visualized successful moments, whether it was launching a new business or completing a significant project. I pictured myself smiling with joy as I saw the results of my efforts, surrounded by people who supported me. Each time I envisioned these moments, I felt a surge of energy and confidence.

The process of visualization became a powerful tool for me. I created vivid pictures in my mind; I saw myself signing a contract with a major client, receiving positive feedback on my work, and watching my business grow. These images gave me additional motivation and the drive to move forward.

Every morning, before starting my day, I would take a few minutes for visualization. I'd take a deep breath, relax, and imagine my goals becoming a reality. This practice helped me stay focused on what truly mattered and not lose sight of my dreams.

I noticed that visualization not only strengthened my motivation, but also helped me overcome fears and doubts. When I saw myself succeeding, it became easier for me to act and make important decisions. I understood that every small victory was a step toward my bigger goals.

This process became more than just a fantasy—it was a real way to strengthen my belief in myself. I learned to trust my abilities and see every failure as an opportunity for growth. Visualizing success opened new horizons for me, and I confidently continued moving forward, knowing that my dreams were not just dreams but goals I could achieve.

Surrounding Myself with Supportive People:
I realized how important it is to surround myself with people who believe in me and support my ambitions. Through this process, I came to understand that success doesn't solely depend on my efforts but also on those around me. I sought to build a circle of people who could inspire me and help me overcome challenges.

My dad played a significant role in this support network. His encouragement meant a great deal to me. I often recalled his words, which echoed like a mantra: "Believing in yourself is the first step to success." These words stayed with me during difficult times when I doubted my abilities. I knew he always believed in me, and that gave me strength.

I began actively seeking out people who shared my passion and vision. These were friends, colleagues, and mentors, each contributing to my journey. I remember once during a meeting with colleagues, we were discussing ideas for a new project. Their enthusiasm and support inspired me to achieve new heights. They shared their experiences and provided valuable advice that helped me grow.

Additionally, I started participating in various groups and communities where people were committed to self-development and supporting each other. This environment became a source of inspiration for me. I saw how interacting with like-minded individuals enriched me and opened new doors.

Whenever I faced difficulties, I remembered the support of my dad and those who stood by me. These memories became a powerful motivator for me. I knew I wasn't alone in my ambitions. Every time I took a step forward, I felt like I had a team behind me, ready to support and help.

Thus, surrounding myself with supportive people became an integral part of my journey to success. It not only helped me overcome challenges but also helped me celebrate my achievements. I learned to value the support I received and sought to share my experiences with others. Now, I understand that my path to success is not only my accomplishment but also the result of those who believed in me and inspired me to achieve new heights.

Continuous Self-Development: I continued to learn and grow despite all the obstacles that stood in my way. This process became not just a necessity but a true passion for me. I understood that to achieve my goals, I not only needed to overcome difficulties but also continually enrich my knowledge and skills.

Reading books became a key part of my education. I immersed myself in literature on self-improvement, business, and psychology. Every book opened new horizons; offering fresh ideas and approaches. I remember coming across a book on leadership, and its advice on inspiring and leading others was a revelation for me. I was eager to apply these insights in my life and work.

Attending courses also played a significant role in my development. I enrolled in online courses and workshops, learning everything from marketing to project management. Each course expanded my knowledge and introduced me to like-minded individuals with whom I could share experiences and receive support. I recall meeting someone in one of these courses who inspired me with his approach to problem-solving. His stories of overcoming difficulties became a model for me.

Learning new skills became a real challenge, but I embraced it as an opportunity. I realized that every new skill brought me closer to my goals. For example, I started learning the basics of programming, which enabled me to understand how digital technologies work in my business. At first, it was difficult, but over time I found enjoyment, which opened up new opportunities for me.

I also became part of various communities where I could exchange experiences and receive advice from more experienced professionals. These connections became a source of support when I doubted my abilities. I learned that you can learn not only in a classroom or through books but also through conversations with others on a similar journey.

Thus, continuous learning and development became an integral part of my life. I learned to see obstacles not as barriers but as opportunities for growth. Every new skill, every book I read, and every course I completed brought me closer to my dreams. Now, I know that the path to success involves never-ending learning - a constant process that makes us better and opens new horizons.

These books can help you better understand yourself, develop personal qualities, and achieve success in different areas of life. I recommend them to everyone:
- **"The Power of Now"** by Eckhart Tolle
  Teaches how to live in the present moment and free yourself from negative thoughts.
- **"Think and Grow Rich"** by Napoleon Hill
  A classic that outlines principles for achieving success and wealth.
- **"The 7 Habits of Highly Effective People"** by Stephen Covey
  A practical guide to personal effectiveness and leadership.
- **"How to Win Friends and Influence People"** by Dale Carnegie
  A textbook on communication and building relationships.
- **"The Power of Habit"** by Charles Duhigg
  Explores how habits are formed and how to change them.
- **"The Miracle Morning"** by Hal Elrod

Recommendations for creating a morning routine for a successful day.
- **"Flow: The Psychology of Optimal Experience"** by Mihaly Csikszentmihalyi
- About the state of flow and its role in achieving happiness and productivity.
- **"Boundaries: When to Say Yes, How to Say No"** by Henry Cloud and John Townsend

  On the importance of setting boundaries in personal and professional life.
- **"You Are a Brand"** by **Catherine Kaputa**

  How to create and develop a personal brand to achieve success.
- **"The Secret"** by Rhonda Byrne

  About the law of attraction and the power of positive thinking.

Conclusion: From Shackles to Freedom
Breaking the shackles of my dreams, I came to an important realization: internal barriers are not just obstacles but real challenges that can and should be overcome. I allowed my fears and doubts to limit me for a long time. Every insecurity felt like an insurmountable wall, pushing me away from my true ambitions and dreams.

But one day, I decided I no longer wanted to be a prisoner of my own thoughts. I began to explore the roots of my doubts. Why didn't I believe in my abilities? Where were these beliefs coming from? Gradually, I realized that many of them were imposed on me from outside—by society, my environment, and my own past failures. I began to understand that if I wanted to move forward, my mindset had to change.

From then on, I started implementing effective strategies to free myself from limiting beliefs. I began simply—by journaling my thoughts and feelings daily. This helped me visualize my fears and see them more objectively. Whenever I encountered a negative thought, I asked myself: "Is this really true?»

 In addition, I started using affirmations—positive statements that helped me build a new perception of myself. I repeated them daily, reminding myself of my abilities and the worthiness of my dreams. These simple but powerful words began to change my inner state.

Over time, I noticed my life changing. I started taking risks that once seemed impossible. I discovered new opportunities that had always been there but were hidden behind the walls of my limitations. I began to believe in my ambitions and in my ability to achieve my dreams.

I understood that overcoming internal barriers is not just the first step toward achieving dreams, but the very process that enriches and develops us. Each victory, no matter how small, strengthened my confidence and inspired me to keep moving forward.

Now I know that your dreams are worth believing in. It is important to remember that each of us has the power to change our perceptions and overcome internal barriers. My experience inspires me, and I hope it will help others find the courage to break their chains and pursue their dreams. Every step on this path is a step toward freedom and self-expression, and it is what leads to true success. It's my hope that my story will free you from your limitation. In the next chapter, we will explore how to formulate your goals to turn them into realistic plans. Stay with us on the path to success!

Chapter 2:
The Magic of Goals: Why Clearly Defined Goals Are More Than Just Words—They're the Key to Your Success

Goals are a powerful tool that turn dreams into actions and ideas into results. I've come to understand that properly formulated goals aren't just empty words; they become my roadmap, creating a structure for success and guiding my efforts in the right direction. In this chapter, I want to share how clearly defined goals can be your key to success, how to set them properly, and the methods to use to achieve them.

The Importance of Properly Defined Goals
Clear goals help you focus on what truly matters. They serve as a guide, keeping you on track and preventing distractions, allowing you to concentrate on your priorities. When I formulate my goals, I ask myself: What do I want to achieve? Why is this important to me? How will this change my life?

Well-set goals are not just tasks; they're a visualization of the future. They help me define where I'm going and motivate me to take action. For example, when I set a goal to open my own business, I'm not just dreaming about the future—I'm creating a concrete action plan to achieve it.

How to Set Goals the Right Way

To ensure that goals are effective, it's essential to follow the SMART principles:
- **S (Specific):** Goals should be specific. Instead of saying, "I want to be successful," say "I want to open an online store by the end of the year."
- **M (Measurable):** Your progress needs to be measurable. For example, "I want to increase my sales by 20% over the next six months."
- **A (Achievable):** Goals should be realistic but ambitious. Make sure they are attainable but still challenging.
- **R (Relevant):** Goals should align with your core values and long-term plans. This will help maintain your motivation.
- **T (Time-bound):** Set a deadline. For example, "I plan to complete a marketing course in three months."

Methods for Achieving Goals

Now that your goals are set, developing a strategy is crucial for achieving

them. Here are a few methods I've found particularly useful:
- **Planning:** Create a detailed plan by breaking the goal into smaller, manageable steps. For example, if your goal is to start a business, the plan might include market research, writing a business plan, and securing funding.
- **Visualization:** Picture yourself achieving your goal. Visualization strengthens your confidence and keeps you motivated.
- **Tracking Progress:** Regularly check in on your achievements. This helps you assess where you are and adjust your actions as needed.
- **Accountability:** Share your goals with others. This creates a sense of responsibility and keeps your motivation strong.
- **Celebrating Milestones:** Don't forget to celebrate your successes, even the small ones. This builds a positive mindset and drives you to keep moving forward.

Overcoming Obstacles

On the road to achieving goals, obstacles are inevitable. It's important to view them as opportunities for growth. When I face challenges, I analyze what I can change in my approach and use it as a chance to learn.
The goals I set act as my compass in life. They help me stay on the right path, act purposefully, and maintain motivation. Turning dreams into actions isn't just about reaching the final result—it's about the process. This can help shape you as a person.

Properly formulated goals are the key to success, opening doors to new opportunities. Each goal is a step toward the life I dream of, and I am ready to keep moving forward, never settling for less.

Part 1: The Essence of Clearly Defined Goals
Goals as a Compass and Roadmap
Clearly defined goals act as a compass, guiding you in the right direction and helping you avoid aimlessness. I've realized that without a clear understanding of my goals, my actions can become chaotic and ineffective. This realization has been key in my journey toward achieving my dreams.

When goals aren't well-defined, it's easy to lose focus. You might take action but not know where those efforts are leading. It's like going on a journey without a map—you can move a lot, but never reach the right destination. Clear goals eliminate uncertainty and create a roadmap to follow.

By defining goals, dreams stop being abstract desires and become practical tasks that need solutions. For instance, instead of just dreaming about opening my own business, I began breaking down the steps necessary to achieve this dream: conducting market research, developing a business plan, building a brand, etc. This transformed my path from a mere wish into a structured process in which I could control my actions.

I also found that clearly written goals help me track my progress. Each achievement, no matter how small, becomes a step towards a larger dream. I started celebrating my successes, which inspired me to keep moving forward. This created a sense of accountability and constant growth, further strengthening my motivation.

A crucial part of this process has been regularly reviewing my goals. I understand that life changes, and sometimes plans need to be adjusted. This flexibility allows me to adapt to new circumstances without losing sight of my main objectives.

Thus, clearly defined goals become more than just words on paper—they become a powerful tool that helps me navigate life and achieve success. They allow me to avoid wandering, act with purpose, and turn dreams into reality. I continue setting new goals, knowing that each one is a step toward the life I dream of.

Example: Steve Jobs and Apple
Steve Jobs had a clear vision of his mission—to revolutionize the world of technology and make it accessible to everyone. His goal was clear: to create innovative products that were not only functional but also beautiful. This vision became the foundation for all strategic decisions at Apple. Because of this, Apple not only achieved success but also fundamentally changed the tech industry.

As Steve Jobs once said,
"Your time is limited, don't waste it living someone else's life. Don't let the noise of others' opinions drown out your inner voice. And most importantly, have the courage to follow your heart and intuition."

Goals and Motivation
Motivation has always played a key role in my pursuit of success. I've noticed that clear goals help maintain high levels of motivation, even when challenges arise. Having a clear goal means working towards something meaningful, which helps me overcome obstacles and stay focused.

When my goal is clear, I feel I'm working towards something significant. This understanding becomes the driving force behind my actions. Clearly formulated goals give meaning to what I do. I remember that when setting a specific goal, such as completing a project or launching a business, I always returned to it during difficult times. This clarity gave me the strength not to give up.

One of the greatest sources of motivation for me was my dad. His support and belief in me were foundational when I was starting out. I remember how he made tools for me to draw and sculpt, emphasizing the importance of creativity in my life. This inspiration gave me the strength to keep pursuing my goals, even when things got tough.

When I faced my first serious challenges, like rejections or failures, I often returned to my goals. I remembered why I started and how much it meant to me and my family. This clarity helped me not give up and to look for solutions. I understood that every step, even the imperfect ones, brought me closer to success.

To maintain a high level of motivation, I used several strategies:

- **Breaking goals into stages:** I divided my larger goals into smaller tasks. For example, when I aimed to get into art school, I broke the process down into steps: preparing a portfolio, studying drawing techniques, and practicing. Each completed step reminded me of my progress.

- **Regular progress review:** I began periodically evaluating my achievements and adjusting my actions. For instance, after every art class, I analyzed what worked and what needed improvement. This kept me on track and focused on my ultimate goal.

- **Visualization of success:** I often imagined how I would feel when I achieved my goals. Visualization helped strengthen my confidence and maintain motivation. I dreamed about my future—working on projects, and making my family proud of my achievements.

- **Seeking support:** I always sought support from friends and colleagues who shared my ambitions. Communicating with people who believed in me helped keep me inspired and motivated.

I realized that motivation can fluctuate. In moments when I lacked inspiration, a sense of discipline became crucial. I understood that success requires consistent effort, and I worked towards my goals even when it was difficult. This strengthened my confidence and showed that persistence pays off.

I learned to celebrate my achievements, even the small ones. When I passed the exams to get into art school, I had a small celebration to mark that important moment. This created a positive cycle: success generated motivation, and motivation helped achieve new goals.

Thus, motivation became an integral part of my journey to success. Clear goals and the support of my loved ones helped me overcome difficulties and stay focused on my dreams. I realized that by setting clear goals and using strategies to achieve them, I move towards my dreams and I grow as a person, which enriches my life experience.

Example: Oprah Winfrey and Her Path to Success
Oprah Winfrey, one of the most influential women in the world, overcame many challenges on her way to success. She always had a clear vision of her goals—to build a successful media empire and become a voice for those who didn't have the opportunity to be heard. This vision was her driving force, helping her overcome obstacles and maintain high motivation throughout her journey.

One of Oprah Winfrey's famous quotes about goals is:
"Success is a result of setting goals and working toward achieving them with belief in yourself."

Part 2: How to Formulate Effective Goals The SMART Method
The SMART method helps formulate goals so they are specific, measurable, achievable, relevant, and time-bound. This method ensures clarity and measurability of goals, allowing you to effectively track progress and adjust actions as needed.

- **Specific:** The goal should be clear and unambiguous. For example, instead of saying, "I want to be successful," say "I want to increase my income by 20% over the next year."

- **Measurable:** Set criteria to measure progress. For instance, instead of saying, "I want to improve my skills," say "I want to complete a project management course and obtain a certification.»

- **Achievable:** Goals should be realistic. Make sure you have the necessary resources and abilities to achieve them. For example, if your goal is to start a business, ensure you have a financing plan and knowledge in that area.

- **Relevant:** Goals should be meaningful and align with your long-term plans. For instance, if you aim for career growth, your goal should be related to professional development.

- **Time-bound:** Set a specific deadline for achieving the goal. For example, "I want to launch a new project by the end of the first quarter."

Example: Elon Musk and SpaceX
Elon Musk uses the SMART method to achieve his ambitious goals. For example, the goal of creating the Falcon 9 rocket was specific (to create a reliable and cost-effective spacecraft), measurable (achieve successful launches), achievable (considering available resources and technologies), relevant (aligned with SpaceX's mission), and time-bound (set a specific date for completion).

Elon Musk once said: "When something is important enough, you do it, even if the odds are against you."

Big goals can seem intimidating. I often faced this feeling when setting ambitious tasks. In such moments, it's easy to get lost in the scale of what's envisioned and start doubting your abilities. However, I quickly realized that breaking down these big goals into smaller sub-goals made them more manageable and realistic.

When I looked at my big goal, like starting my own business, it seemed too complex and distant. However, breaking this goal into sub-goals made them feel more achievable. For example, the first sub-goal could be market research, the second—writing a business plan, and the third—securing financing. Each of these steps felt more real and doable.

Breaking big goals into sub-goals allows you to focus on short-term tasks that bring you closer to the main goal. I began setting specific, measurable tasks to accomplish within a week or a month. This gave me a sense of progress and success as I achieved these sub-goals. Each completed step strengthened my motivation and belief in my abilities.

Moreover, sub-goals help structure the process of achieving larger goals

They serve as a roadmap that guide my actions. I created task lists, and as I checked off each completed sub-goal, I felt myself moving closer to my ultimate objective. This made planning easier and my journey more understandable and organized.

Breaking down goals into sub-goals also allows for regular progress evaluation. I started tracking how far I had come and what steps were still needed. This not only helped me see the results of my efforts but also allowed me to adjust my plans if something wasn't going as expected. I could adapt and find new solutions, which significantly increased my chances of success.

Each time I reached one of my sub-goals, it became a small celebration. I learned to acknowledge my achievements, which created a positive mindset and additional motivation. These successes, even if small, fueled my journey forward.

Thus, breaking down big goals into sub-goals is a powerful tool that simplifies the path to success. Sub-goals make large tasks more manageable, help focus on short-term results, and allow for progress assessment. I realized that by breaking my dreams into smaller and more achievable steps, I move closer to my goal and I enjoy the process. This makes the path to success not only clearer but more inspiring.

Example: J.K. Rowling and the Creation of Harry Potter

J.K. Rowling started with the goal of writing a book about Harry Potter. Her goal was broken down into sub-goals: creating the world of Harry Potter, developing characters, writing chapters, editing the text, and so on. Each of these sub-goals made writing the book more structured and achievable.

Part 3: Overcoming Obstacles on the Way to Goals
Motivation and Persistence

Achieving goals can be difficult, especially when facing obstacles. Maintaining motivation and persistence is the key to overcoming barriers. Regularly reviewing your progress will help you stay focused and adjust your course when necessary.

Example: Thomas Edison and the Light Bulb

Thomas Edison's name has become synonymous with innovation and invention. One of his most famous inventions is the incandescent light bulb, which forever changed how we think about lighting and everyday life. However the creation of this bulb was not a simple journey and was filled with challenges.

Edison began working on the incandescent bulb in 1878, aiming to create a practical and long-lasting light source. Before him, various forms of lighting existed, such as gas lamps and candles, but they were inconvenient and unsafe. Edison dreamed of a reliable and efficient solution that could provide light in homes and streets.

The road to success was not easy. Edison conducted thousands of experiments, testing various materials for the filament. He tried numerous substances, including carbon, iron, and even plant fibers. Despite many failures, Edison did not give up. His famous quote, "I have not failed. I've just found 10,000 ways that won't work," perfectly illustrates his persistence and determination.

Finally, in 1879, Edison made a breakthrough by creating a carbon filament that effectively glowed when an electric current passed through it. This material proved durable and robust enough to be used in lamps. Edison received a patent for his invention and began producing incandescent bulbs in large quantities.

With the invention of the incandescent bulb, the world of lighting changed forever. Edison founded a company that began mass-producing light bulbs and developed an electrical lighting network, providing reliable light sources for cities and homes. Incandescent bulbs became an integral part of everyday life, significantly improving the quality of life for many.

Edison's work on the incandescent light bulb became a symbol of persistence and innovation. His approach to experimentation, his willingness to learn from failure, and his drive for perfection inspired many future inventors and entrepreneurs. Edison created technology that changed the world and laid the foundation for the development of electrical engineering and science in general.

Thomas Edison and his incandescent light bulb is a story of how determination and innovation can change society. Edison proved that even the most ambitious ideas can become reality if you don't fear difficulties and persistently move toward your goal. His legacy continues to inspire us, reminding us of the importance of perseverance and belief in our ideas.

Learning from Mistakes

Mistakes and failures can become valuable sources of learning. It's important to analyze your mistakes and use the lessons learned to adjust actions and improve strategy.

Example: Warren Buffett and His Investments

Warren Buffett, one of the most well-known and successful investors, is not only a master of investments but also an example of how mistakes and failures can be used as powerful learning tools. His approach to investing is rooted in constant self-improvement and analyzing his mistakes, helping him make more informed decisions and achieve greater success.

Buffett is never ashamed to talk about his failures. He understands that mistakes are an integral part of the learning process. In his interviews and Annual Letters to Shareholders, he openly shares examples of his failed investments. Acknowledging mistakes allows him to analyze what went wrong and to share his experience with others, showing that even the most successful people face difficulties.

For Buffett, every mistake is an opportunity for growth. He approaches each failure with an analytical mindset, trying to understand the causes that led to it. For example, he has shared experiences of failed investments in companies that turned out to be overvalued or had weak business models. These lessons help him better evaluate potential investments in the future.

Buffett uses his mistakes to improve his investment strategy. He actively revises his approaches and methodologies to avoid repeating the same mistakes. For example, he has become more cautious in selecting companies, focusing on financial stability and long-term prospects rather than short-term profits.

Another important lesson Buffett learned from his mistakes is the necessity of emotional control. He emphasizes that a successful investor must remain calm and not panic during market fluctuations. This allows him to make rational decisions based on facts, not emotions.

Buffett learns from his mistakes and actively shares his experience with young investors. He frequently speaks at seminars and conferences, sharing his views on investments, business, and life in general. This demonstrates his commitment to passing on knowledge and helping others on their own investment journeys.

Warren Buffett is an example of how mistakes can be used as a tool for learning and improvement. His approach to failure shows that true success lies not only in achieving goals but also in the ability to learn along the way. Buffett reminds us that every failure can be a crucial step toward greater success if we are willing to analyze our mistakes and learn from them. This makes him a great investor and a wise mentor to many.

Part 4: Tools and Techniques for Achieving Goals

Visualization

I have found that visualization is a powerful tool that helps me picture myself achieving my goals. When I create vivid and detailed images of how I achieve my objectives, it not only inspires me but also significantly boosts my motivation and focus.

When I start visualizing my goals, I try to make the image as vivid as possible. I close my eyes and dive into the details: what feelings I am experiencing, what I see around me, and what sounds surround me. For example, when I dreamed of starting my own business, I imagined what my office would look like, how I would interact with clients, and how I would feel when my ideas started bringing success. These images fill me with energy and inspiration.

Visualization helps me stay motivated, especially when the road to my goal becomes difficult. When I encounter obstacles, I return to my vivid images. This reminds me why I am working so hard and pushes me to keep going. I understand that each effort brings me closer to the picture I see in my mind.

Creating detailed images helps me focus on specific actions I need to take to achieve my goal. I start breaking down my big goals into smaller tasks and visualize myself successfully completing them. This allows me to see the final result and understand what needs to be done at each stage. I act with confidence, in the knowledge that I have a clear plan.

Visualization also helps me cultivate a positive mindset. It helps me learn to believe in myself, and that achieving my goal is possible. When I picture myself in a successful role, it changes my perception of reality. I begin acting like someone who has already achieved their goal, which gives me confidence and determination.

I have realized that visualization is not a one-time process but a regular practice. I try to set aside time each day, to immerse myself in my images and dreams. This helps me maintain focus and inspiration, as well as adapt to changes and new challenges along the way to my goals.

Thus, visualization has become an important tool in my pursuit of goals. It has shown me that creating vivid and detailed images can help increase motivation and concentration. This process inspires me and also allows me to move more purposefully toward my dreams. Visualization reminds me that I am capable of more and that each step brings me closer to the desired result.

Example: Michael Jordan and Visualization

Michael Jordan, the legendary basketball player and one of the greatest athletes in history, used visualization as a crucial tool for enhancing his skills and preparing for games. His approach to visualization helped him achieve outstanding results on the court and cope with the pressure that comes with performing at a high level.

Jordan often imagined various game scenarios that could arise during matches. He would close his eyes and vividly visualize himself dribbling the ball, driving past defenders, and making shots from different positions and in various conditions. This practice helped him mentally rehearse possible situations in advance, making him more confident and prepared for any surprises on the court.

Visualization also played a significant role in his training process. Jordan would picture himself performing different drills — from simple shots to complex moves. He used this method to fine-tune his skills and improve his technique. This approach not only allowed him to see how he would execute the drills but also to feel how his body would move, which increased the effectiveness of his training.

Visualization helped Jordan manage the psychological pressure that comes before important games. He would imagine stepping onto the court, hearing the crowd's cheers, feeling the tension, yet remaining calm and focused. This practice enabled him to reduce stress levels and boost his confidence, which ultimately reflected in his performance.

Even when Jordan faced difficulties, he used visualization to regain his motivation. For example, after a tough game or missing a crucial shot, he would return to his images of success and see himself as a winner once again. This ability to visualize himself on top helped him overcome failures and keep moving forward.

Jordan's approach to visualization became an example for many athletes and individuals in other fields. He demonstrated that mental preparation is just as important as physical training. Visualization has become an integral part of the training process for many athletes striving for success.

Michael Jordan used visualization as a powerful tool, which contributed to his remarkable achievements on the court. Creating vivid images of game situations and training drills helped him develop his skills, manage pressure, and maintain confidence in his abilities. His experience shows that visualization is not just a technique but a philosophy that can transform one's approach to achieving goals and overcoming challenges.

Using Planners and Apps

In today's world, technology plays a key role in how we interact with tasks and goals daily. There are many tools available that help plan and track goals efficiently, ensuring organization and productivity. I personally use these technologies and see how they simplify the process of achieving what I set out to do.

Planners, both traditional paper ones and digital ones, provide a convenient way to structure tasks and goals. I prefer using digital planners, which allow for easy updates and adjustments. With their help, I can break down my larger goals into smaller tasks, set deadlines, and track my progress. This helps me stay focused on important steps toward achieving my objectives.

There are many apps specifically designed for goal setting and tracking. I use several that offer different features — from reminders to progress charts. For example, some apps allow me to set SMART goals (Specific, Measurable, Achievable, Relevant, Time-bound) and monitor how close I am to achieving them. This gives me confidence and helps me stay focused on my tasks.

Tools for tracking progress, such as spreadsheets and charts, allow me to visualize my achievements. I love seeing how my efforts lead to results; visual reminders motivate me to continue working toward my goals. Trackers help not only to monitor successes but also to identify areas that need more attention.

Calendar apps are another important tool in my arsenal. I use them to schedule important events, deadlines, and meetings. This helps me manage my time effectively and avoid scheduling conflicts. Synchronization across devices allows me to stay up-to-date with all my commitments, no matter where I am.

The in-app reminder feature helps ensure that I don't forget important tasks and events. I set notifications to appear at the right time, reminding me of upcoming deadlines or meetings. This significantly reduces the chances of missing something important and helps me stay organized.

Modern technology provides numerous tools for planning and tracking goals. Using planners, apps, progress trackers, and calendars helps me stay organized and efficient. These technologies simplify the process of achieving goals and make it more engaging and visually stimulating. I realize that by using these tools, I significantly increase my chances of success and achieve desired results faster and with less effort.

Example: Tim Ferriss and His Tools

Tim Ferriss, author of the bestseller The 4-Hour Workweek, has become a symbol of effective time management and work optimization. In his book and other materials, he shares methods and tools that help him achieve goals and increase productivity. I find his approaches inspiring and apply some of them in my own life.

Ferriss advocates for minimalism in work. He believes there's no need to overload yourself with numerous tasks when you can focus on the important ones. He suggests using the 80/20 rule (the Pareto Principle), which states that 20% of efforts bring 80% of results. This approach helps me identify the most significant tasks and optimize my workflow.

Tim actively uses planners to structure his time and tasks. He prefers digital tools like note-taking and task-organizing apps, which allow him to quickly make changes and track progress. I also use planners to break down large projects into smaller tasks and keep track of their completion.

Ferriss shares a variety of technologies that help him automate routine processes. For example, he uses time-management apps like Pomodoro timers, which help him stay focused on tasks for set periods. I've found that these tools help me avoid procrastination and increase concentration.

One of the key aspects of Ferriss's philosophy is task delegation. He argues that it's important to learn how to hand over some responsibilities to others to focus on more critical matters. I've begun applying this approach in my own life by hiring assistants or using freelancers for tasks that don't require my direct involvement.

Ferriss also recommends keeping journals to track thoughts and ideas. This helps him analyze his achievements and identify areas for improvement. I've found that journaling allows me to better understand my goals and progress, as well as maintain motivation.

Tim Ferriss demonstrates how planners and modern tools can significantly boost productivity and efficiency. His approaches to minimalism, task delegation, and the use of technology inspire me to optimize my work process. By applying his methods, I see how I can achieve my goals faster and with less effort, allowing me to enjoy life and devote more time to what truly matters.

Clearly defined goals represent a powerful tool that can direct your efforts and resources in the right direction. Setting goals using the SMART method, breaking them down into sub-goals, maintaining motivation, and learning from mistakes will help you effectively achieve your objectives. Visualization and modern tools also play a crucial role in goal attainment. By utilizing these methods and techniques, you can set clear goals and accomplish them.

Tracking progress and maintaining motivation are essential components of successfully reaching goals. By applying the described methods and examples, you can create an effective tracking and support system that will help keep you on the right path. Regular reports, visualization, rewards, and support from your environment will all contribute to achieving your goals and maintaining a high level of motivation throughout the journey.

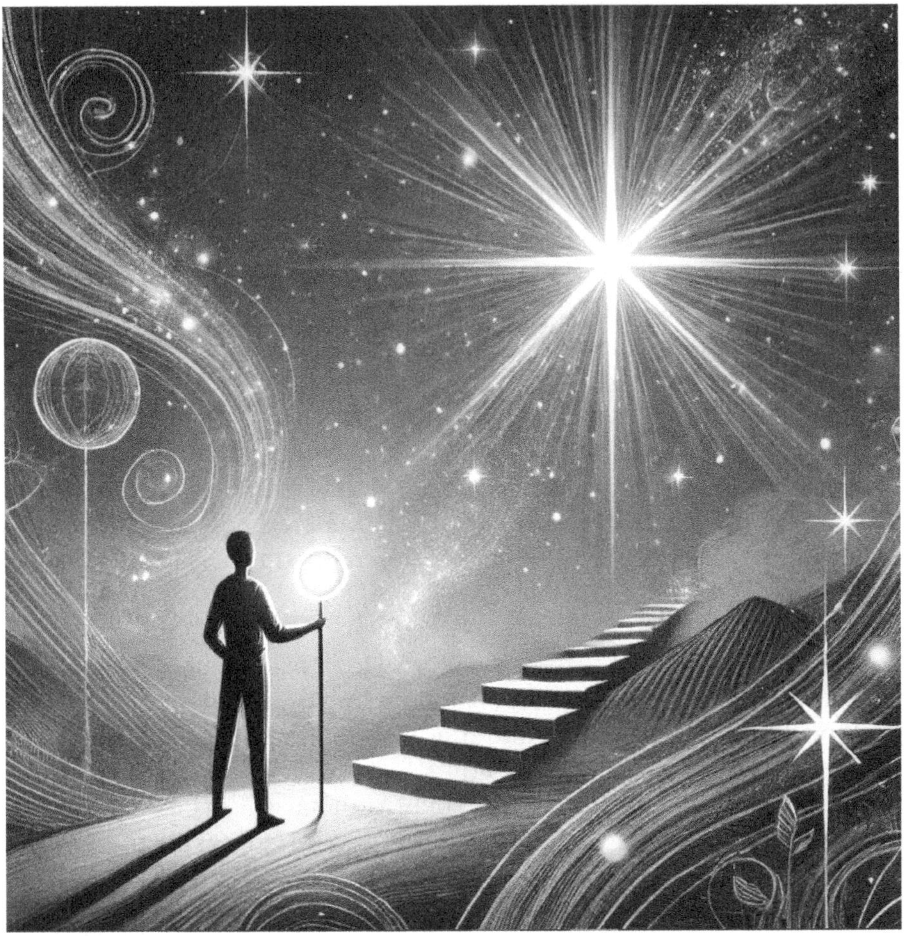

Chapter 3:
Creating a Dream: How to Visualize Your Dreams to Turn Them into an Action Plan

Visualization is a powerful tool that helps transform abstract dreams into concrete plans and actions. In this chapter, we'll discuss how to visualize your dreams, so they're not only in your imagination, but real achievements. I will share my personal example to demonstrate how vivid and inspiring images of the future can guide you on your path to success.

The Importance of Visualization Visualization as a Goal-Achieving Tool

Visualization is not just the process of imagining; it's about creating a detailed and vivid picture of your desired future. When you clearly envision what you want to achieve, you create a powerful internal drive that pushes you toward your goals.

Example from My Life: The Road to Becoming a Designer

When I first started my design journey, I had a clear dream of what I wanted to become. I envisioned myself in prestigious studios, working on projects that inspired people. These images became my goals and served as a source of motivation.

From the very beginning, I started visualizing my future. I pictured myself working in a creative team where ideas and concepts come to life. I dreamed of my own projects—logos, web design, and marketing materials. Every time I returned to these images, I felt inspired and knew I wanted to keep moving forward.

I understood that achieving my dream required knowledge and skills. So, I decided to enroll in a design college. Preparing for exams, studying the works of other designers, and creating my portfolio became part of my daily routine. I visualized myself as a student immersed in the atmosphere of creativity and learning. After successfully getting admitted, I fully dove into my studies.

Each project allowed me to showcase my abilities and develop my skills. I seized every opportunity to work on real assignments and imagined how these experiences would help me in the future.

After college, I realized I wasn't done yet. I enrolled in a design academy to deepen my knowledge. Continuing to visualize myself in this new role, I pictured myself surrounded by talented teachers and peers. At the academy, I was determined. Every project and task brought me closer to my dream.

I not only learned from my professors but also from my fellow students. As I completed my work, I imagined how they would be received. This inspired me to keep moving forward.

At every stage, I continued to visualize my future. I imagined creating inspiring projects that would impact the market. I dreamed of recognition and the chance to share my experience with others. This practice reinforced my motivation and helped me develop a strategy for achieving my goals.

I attended workshops, participated in competitions, and sought out opportunities for growth. Whenever challenges arose, I returned to my images of success, which served as a source of inspiration.

My path in design was the result of combining visualization and persistence. I began with vivid images of the future and, step by step, moved closer to my dream—studying, working, and growing. This practice helped me realize my ambitions and showed the importance of believing in yourself. I continue to visualize my future, which gives me the strength to push forward, striving for new heights in design.

How Visualization Works

Visualization activates your motivation and focus, helping your brain find solutions and resources to achieve your goal. A clear picture of the end result helps you stay on track, overcome challenges, and adjust your actions as needed.

Example: Steve Jobs and Apple

Steve Jobs, co-founder of Apple, was known not only for his charisma and leadership qualities but also for his unique approach to visualization. He understood that to achieve greatness for his company, it was necessary to have a clear vision of the future and how his innovative products would change the world of technology.

Jobs actively used visualization to imagine how Apple could change people's approach to technology. He often created vivid images of products that not only performed their functions but also became integral parts of people's lives. Whether it was the Mac, iPhone, or iPad, he saw them not just as devices, but as tools capable of inspiring and improving life.

Visualization allowed Jobs to focus on Apple's long-term goals. He dreamed of making Apple synonymous with innovation and quality. These images helped him shape the company's development strategy and inspire his team. He knew how to share his visions with employees, motivating them to work on projects with the same level of enthusiasm and ambition.

By creating a clear vision of the future, Jobs was able to effectively guide his team's efforts toward realizing that dream. He understood that each project and every new idea had to serve the overall goal—revolutionizing the technology industry. His visualization was not just a dream but a concrete action plan that motivated those around him.

This ability to visualize the future and imagine how his products would be perceived by users played a key role in creating many innovative solutions. Jobs didn't just offer technology—he created an ecosystem in which products worked harmoniously and changed the established order.

Steve Jobs used visualization as a powerful tool for achieving Apple's ambitious goals. His vivid images of the future inspired his team and also helped them focus on strategic objectives. Jobs proved that a clear vision and the ability to imagine how your ideas will change the world can become the foundation for true revolutions in the industry.

Practical Steps to Visualizing Dreams
Here's how you can begin visualizing your dreams effectively:

1. Create a vivid mental image of your dream, paying attention to the details. Imagine yourself in the future, having already achieved your goals.
2. Engage your senses during visualization: What do you see, hear, feel in this future? Make the vision as real as possible.
3. Visualize daily. Spend time each day imagining your goals as already achieved.
4. Write down your vision. Put your dreams into words to help make them more tangible.
5. Use visualization to overcome obstacles. When challenges arise, return

to your vision to remind yourself of the bigger picture and inspire perseverance. By applying these techniques, you can turn your dreams into concrete plans and take steps toward making them a reality.

Step 1: Defining Your Dreams

Before starting visualization, it's important to clearly define what you want to achieve. Write down your dreams and goals. This will help you create a clear vision of what you want to see in your future.

When I decided to open my own advertising agency, I detailed what I wanted to accomplish. I wrote down how I wanted my office to look, the types of clients I would have, and the projects I would work on. This helped me form a clear picture of the future.

Step 2: Creating Vivid Images

Create detailed and vivid images of your success. It's important that these images are lively and specific.

Include not only the visual aspect but also the emotions you'll feel when achieving your goals.

I envisioned myself sitting in my office, surrounded by creative colleagues, discussing new projects. I saw how my office looked, how clients came for meetings, and how we launched successful ad campaigns. These images were so vivid that they inspired me daily.

Step 3: Using Mind Maps and Visual Tools

Use mind maps and visual boards to solidify your images. These can include drawings, photos, magazine clippings, or collages that represent your goals and dreams.

I created a vision board where I placed images of successful advertising campaigns, photos of my future office, and inspiring quotes. This board helped me see what I was striving for and kept my motivation high.

Step 4: Regular Visualization and Meditation

Make time for regular visualization and meditation. Picture yourself achieving your goals and experience those moments with full emotional intensity.

Every morning, I took a few minutes to visualize my goals. I imagined how my company was growing, signing contracts, and how our projects were yielding results. These morning sessions helped me stay focused and maintain high levels of motivation.

Step 5: Updating and Adjusting Goals

Over time, your dreams and goals may evolve. It's important to regularly review and adjust your visions and plans to match your current situation and ambitions.

As my advertising agency grew, I revisited and adjusted my goals. I added new projects, expanded services, and adapted the strategy in response to market changes and new opportunities.

Maria, a Sports Psychologist
Maria is a sports psychologist who works with clients looking to improve their athletic performance. Her morning visualization sessions follow a specific structure to help set her up for a successful day.

Every morning, Maria wakes up at 6:00 a.m. and immediately sits on a meditation cushion in a quiet corner of her home. She begins deep breathing to calm her mind and prepare for the day. Then, with her eyes closed, she starts visualizing successful sessions with her clients.

She imagines how her clients, starting from hesitant individuals, become confident and achieve remarkable results. She sees them overcoming mental barriers and reaching goals that once seemed unattainable. Maria focuses on the details: hearing positive feedback from clients, seeing their smiles, and witnessing the joy from their accomplishments.

This process takes her about 10 minutes. After her visualization session, she feels more confident and motivated, ready for the day's meetings and challenges. This method has helped her improve her professional practice and strengthen her clients' trust.

Dmitry, an Antique Restorer
Dmitry, an antique restorer, begins each day with a visualization session to prepare for the successful completion of his projects. His morning ritual starts with rising early, ensuring he has time for himself before diving into work.

He sits in his workshop, surrounded by tools and work samples, and closes his eyes. Dmitry visualizes working on a complex project, such as restoring an old mirror or painting. He sees his hands carefully and meticulously restoring the details, making the object even more valuable and beautiful.

Dmitry focuses on the end result—an impeccably restored piece that amazes clients and collectors alike. He also visualizes his work receiving recognition at exhibitions and in professional circles.

These morning visualization sessions help Dmitry improve the quality of his work and attract new clients who are impressed by his craftsmanship and attention to detail.

Olga, a Startup Founder
Olga, the founder of a tech startup, uses morning visualization sessions to create a clear picture of her business's future. Every morning, she wakes up early and finds a quiet space to focus on her goals.

She begins by closing her eyes and visualizing a successful business: her startup gaining the attention of investors, receiving positive customer reviews, and becoming a market leader. Olga imagines her team working in harmony, her ideas turning into successful products, and the company expanding into international markets.

She pays attention to details: hearing congratulations from investors, seeing customer appreciation, and feeling pride in the results achieved. These visualization sessions help her reinforce confidence in her business and act with greater focus in her daily tasks.

Ivan, a Yoga Instructor
Ivan, a yoga instructor, uses morning visualization sessions to prepare for his classes and increase his effectiveness as a teacher. He wakes up early and takes time for meditation and visualization.

Each morning, he closes his eyes and envisions his classes going perfectly. He sees his students practicing yoga, reaching harmony, and improving their physical and mental well-being. Ivan focuses on seeing his students smile, relax, and enjoy the practice.

This process helps Ivan maintain a positive attitude and prepare for his classes, improving the quality of his teaching and creating a more comfortable atmosphere for his students.

Alena, a Writer
Alena, a writer, uses morning visualization sessions to prepare for the success of her literary projects. Every morning, she wakes up early and spends 10 minutes in a quiet place, focusing on her thoughts.

She begins by closing her eyes and visualizing her book becoming a bestseller. Alena imagines her work receiving positive reviews from critics, readers sharing their impressions, and her book topping sales charts. She also visualizes successful book tours and meetings with readers.

This practice helps Alena strengthen her belief in her abilities and sets a productive tone for the day when she starts writing. Natalia, a Choreographer Natalia, a choreographer, uses morning visualization sessions to prepare for successful performances and rehearsals. Every morning, she wakes up early and finds time to focus on her goals.

She closes her eyes and visualizes her dance groups winning competitions and gaining recognition.
Natalia imagines her students performing brilliantly, with audiences and judges being impressed by their skills. She also sees her choreography gaining popularity and inspiring others.

 This practice helps Natalia stay positive and create successful dance performances that receive praise and recognition.

Visualization and Action
Turning Visualization into Concrete Actions

Visualization is just the beginning. It's essential to translate your images into specific actions. Identify the steps you need to take to achieve your goals and start taking action.

After visualizing the successful growth of my advertising agency, I developed a concrete action plan. I defined growth stages, hired key employees, and began seeking clients. This helped me turn my dreams into reality.

Tracking Progress and Maintaining Motivation

Keep track of your progress and celebrate your achievements. This will help you stay motivated and ensure you're on the right path.

I regularly reviewed the results of my agency's work. I noted successful projects, achieved goals, and gathered client feedback. This allowed me to see that we were moving in the right direction and motivated me to continue working toward new objectives.

Tracking Progress and Maintaining Motivation

Tracking progress and maintaining motivation are key aspects of achieving any goal. Without a clear understanding of how you are advancing and without mechanisms to support your motivation, the drive towards your goals can quickly wane. In this chapter, we will explore how to effectively track your progress and maintain a high level of motivation. We will analyze various strategies and methods that can help you stay on the right path to success.

1. Defining Key Metrics

To make progress tracking effective, it's essential to define key metrics that reflect your success. These can be specific indicators such as sales volume, the number of completed tasks, or levels of achieved results. For instance, if your goal is to increase sales by 20% over a quarter, key metrics might include weekly sales, conversion rates, average transaction value, and the number of new customers. Regularly monitoring these indicators will allow you to see how close you are to your goal and where potential issues may arise.

Method:
- Set clear and measurable goals. Break down the overall goal into specific steps.
- Choose relevant metrics. These metrics should directly reflect your progress.
- Regularly collect data. Use spreadsheets, charts, or specialized software.

2. Using Tools and Technologies
Modern technology provides powerful tools for tracking progress. Applications and software can significantly simplify this process. Project management tools like Asana, Trello, or Monday.com allow you to track task completion, set deadlines, and receive progress notifications. These tools enable you to visualize your progress and make timely adjustments.

Method:

Method:
- Choose a suitable tool based on your needs and preferences.
- Set up your project and tasks. Break your goal down into individual tasks and set deadlines.
- Regularly update the status. Periodically check and adjust the information.

3. Regular Reports and Reviews

Reports and reviews allow for systematic assessment of your progress and identification of potential problems.

Many successful companies conduct weekly or monthly performance reports. This not only helps track achievements but also enables timely identification of deviations from the plan and prompt responses.

Method:
- Determine the frequency of reports. This can be weekly, monthly, or another period that suits you.
- Collect and analyze data using pre-defined metrics.
- Conclude and make adjustments. Discuss the results and plan the next steps.

4. Setting Short-Term Goals and Sub-Goals

Dividing the main goal into short-term goals and sub-goals makes it easier to track progress and maintain motivation. If your goal is to complete a large project in six months, set short-term goals such as completing key phases every two months. This will allow you to see results at each stage and not lose motivation.

Method:
- Break down the main goal into sub-goals. Identify key milestones and deadlines.
- Establish criteria for each sub-goal. Ensure they are measurable.
- Regularly check the completion of sub-goals. Adjust the plan as necessary.

5. Using Visual Techniques

Visualizing progress helps you see how far you have come and supports motivation. Creating charts, diagrams, or tables to track progress allows you to see results visually. For example, many people use calendars to mark days when they completed tasks or charts that display goal achievements.

Method:
- Create visual tools such as charts, graphs, or other visualization methods.
- Regularly update visual elements to reflect achieved results and progress.
- Use visualization for motivation. Clear results can serve as a source of inspiration.

6. Self-Assessment and Feedback

Self-assessment and receiving feedback from others help you evaluate your progress more objectively. Regular self-assessment allows you to understand how close you are to achieving your goals and where improvement is needed. Feedback from colleagues or mentors provides a fresh perspective on your progress and helps identify areas for growth.

Method:
- Conduct regular self-assessments. Evaluate your achievements and identify areas for improvement.
- Request feedback. Ask colleagues, mentors, or clients to assess your work.
- Analyze and apply the feedback. Use the information gained to adjust your plan.

7. Motivation Through Rewards Rewards

for achieving goals help maintain motivation and strengthen the drive for success. Many successful individuals set personal rewards for achieving intermediate goals. For example, if you reach a significant milestone in a project, you might treat yourself to something enjoyable to celebrate your success.

Method:
- Define rewards that will motivate you.
- Set conditions for receiving the reward. For instance, completing a specific project phase.
- Celebrate achievements. Enjoy the reward and use it as additional motivation

8. Adaptation and Flexibility

Being flexible and ready to adapt your plans based on changes and new circumstances is crucial. Sometimes it becomes necessary to change a plan due to unexpected problems or new opportunities. Flexibility allows you to respond promptly and adjust your course.

Method:
- Periodically review your plan. Assess the need for changes.
- Be prepared to adapt. Make changes to the plan according to new conditions.
- Evaluate the results of adaptations. Analyze the effectiveness of the changes made.

9. Support from Your Environment
Support from friends, family, and colleagues plays an important role in maintaining motivation and tracking progress. Discussing your goals with loved ones or colleagues helps sustain motivation and gain support. For example, family involvement in planning and celebrating achievements contributes to more significant progress.

Method:
- Share your goals with those around you. Open up about your plans and progress.
- Seek support. Look for advice and assistance from friends and family.
- Celebrate achievements together. Share successes with others.

10. Continuous Learning and Development
Learning and developing new skills help maintain motivation and improve results. Regular learning, attending training sessions, or courses can help you acquire new skills that positively influence goal achievement. For instance, participating in personal effectiveness workshops can enhance your motivational strategies.

Method:
- Look for learning opportunities. Identify areas for development.
- Participate in training sessions and courses. Enroll in learning programs on topics of interest.
- Apply new knowledge in practice. Implement the skills you've acquired into your goals and tasks.

Visualization of dreams is not just a method; it's a process that helps you create a vivid and inspiring representation of the future. Clear imagery, regular visualization sessions, and translating them into specific actions will help direct your energy and resources towards achieving your goals. My personal experience shows how vivid images and clear plans have transformed into the successful development of an advertising agency; I'm confident that with these methods, you too can achieve your dreams. Let me know if you need any changes or further assistance!

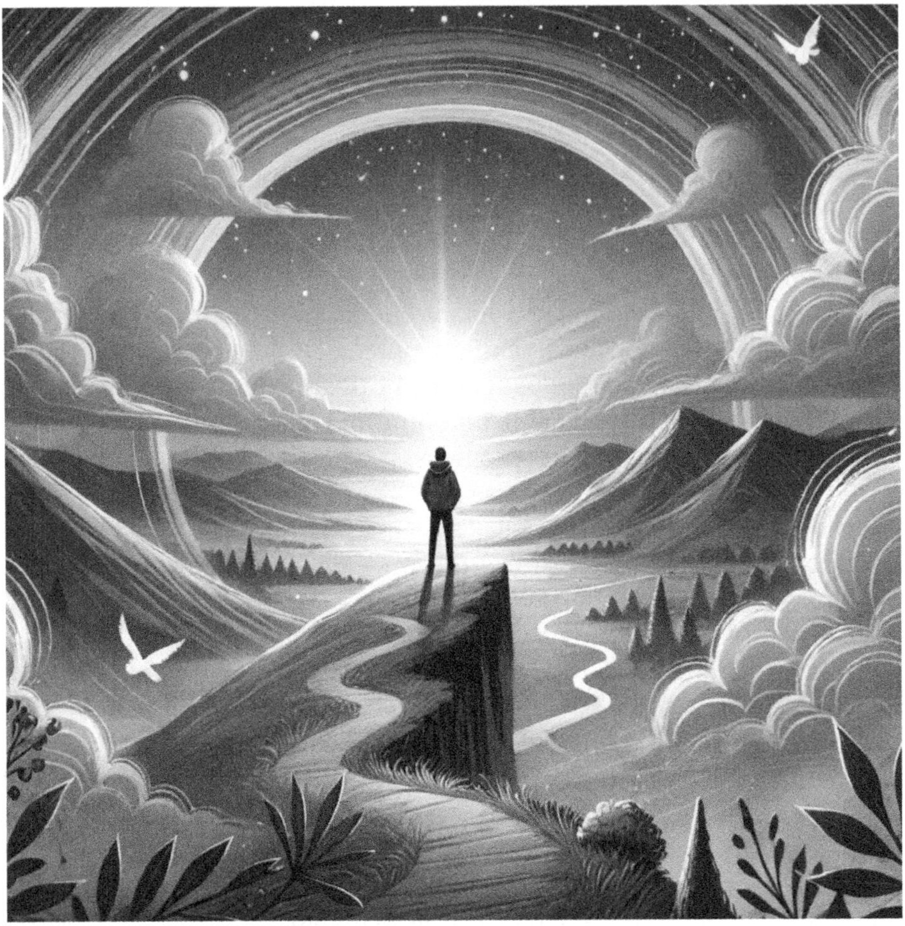

Chapter 4:
Mapping Your Path

Creating a roadmap is not just planning; it's the art of transforming your dreams into a structured and actionable plan. This chapter is dedicated to the step-by-step process of creating a roadmap that will guide you on the path to success. We will explore how to turn abstract dreams and ambitions into a realistic action plan, helping you move towards your goals.

1. Defining the End Goal

Step 1: Formulate Your End Goal
Before you start creating a roadmap, it's important to clearly define your end goal. This should be a specific and measurable objective you aim to achieve.
For example, if you want to open your own business, your end goal might be stated as, "Open and launch a successful online store within 12 months." This clear description of your goal gives you an understanding of the end result you are striving for.

Methodology:
- Use the SMART method. Ensure your goal is Specific, Measurable, Achievable, Relevant, and Time-bound.
- Describe the goal in detail. Include all aspects that will help you understand what achieving the goal means.
- Write down the goal. Use notes or a document to record and visualize your goal.

2. Breaking the Goal into Subgoals

Step 2: Identify Subgoals
- Break down your end goal into smaller subgoals that will help you achieve the main goal. These subgoals should be specific steps you need to take.
- For opening an online store, subgoals might include:
- Conducting market and competitor research.
- Developing a business plan.
- Creating and launching a website.
- Developing a marketing and advertising strategy.
- Assembling a team and handling legal documentation.

Methodology:
- Make a list of subgoals. Identify all key steps that need to be completed.
- Set deadlines for each subgoal. Determine when each subgoal should be achieved.
- Assign responsibilities. Specify who will be responsible for completing each subgoal.

3. Creating a Detailed Action Plan

Step 3: Develop a Detailed Plan

Each subgoal requires a more detailed action plan. This plan should include specific tasks, deadlines, and resources.

For the subgoal "Develop a business plan," your action plan might include:
- Conducting market research and analysis.
- Defining the business model and revenue streams.
- Preparing a financial plan.
- Writing and editing the document.
- Seeking feedback from consultants.

Methodology:
- Break down subgoals into tasks. Establish specific actions that need to be performed.
- Identify resources. Specify what resources (time, money, materials) will be needed to complete the tasks.
- Assign deadlines. Set realistic deadlines for each task.

4. Monitoring and Adjusting the Plan

Step 4: Establish a Monitoring System

- Effective execution of the plan requires regular monitoring of progress and making adjustments.
- If you notice that creating the website takes longer than expected, you may need to revisit the deadlines or allocate resources more efficiently. Regular check-ins will help you identify and resolve issues promptly.

Methodology:
- Set a frequency for check-ins. This could be weekly, monthly, or at another convenient interval.
- Use monitoring tools. Implement software for tracking task and plan completion.
- Evaluate progress. Compare actual results against the planned ones and make necessary changes.

5. Using Visual Tools

Step 5: Visualize Your Plan
- Visual tools will help you understand and follow your plan.
- Creating Gantt charts or visual roadmaps will allow you to see the stages of task completion and progress in each of them. Such tools will help you maintain organization and focus.

Methodology:
- Choose a visual tool. Use charts, graphs, calendar plans, or specialized applications.
- Visualize the plan. Highlight important dates, tasks, and subgoals.
- Regularly update visual tools. Display achieved results and progress. Visualizing the plan is a crucial step toward successfully achieving your goals. This process helps you see what your path to success will look like and how different steps and stages will interact. In this part, I will share how I applied visualization to achieve my goals and how you can use this approach to enhance your effectiveness.

Defining Goals and Stages

Example from Personal Practice:
When I decided to open my advertising agency, I began by creating a clear visual representation of my plan. My end goal was clear: "Launch a successful advertising agency within 12 months." To make this goal more manageable, I broke it down into several key stages.

Methodology:

Recording Goals and Subgoals. I wrote down each of the subgoals that needed to be achieved, such as "Market Research," "Business Plan Development," "Website Creation," etc.

Creating a Timeline. I allocated time periods for each subgoal and marked them on my calendar.

Using Visual Tools

Example from Personal Practice:
To visualize my plan, I used a Gantt chart. This helped me clearly see how various tasks overlapped and depended on one another.

Methodology:
- Creating a Gantt Chart. I created a Gantt chart in Excel, where I listed tasks, deadlines, and responsible individuals for each task. This allowed me to easily track progress.
- Using Color Coding. Different stages and tasks were marked with various colors to visually highlight their priority and completion status.

Visualizing Processes and Resources

Example from Personal Practice:
To understand what resources I would need, I created visual maps showing resource allocation across projects. I also used flowcharts to depict workflows and the interactions of various parts of the business.

Methodology:
- Creating Flowcharts. I drew flowcharts illustrating the main processes in the agency, such as client acquisition, advertising campaign development, and reporting.
- Resource Allocation. I used charts to visualize the distribution of budget, time, and other resources across projects.

Regularly Updating Visualizations

Example from Personal Practice:
My plan and visualizations were not static. I regularly updated the Gantt chart and flowcharts to reflect current changes and achievements. This helped me stay on course and make necessary adjustments.

Methodology:
- **Updating Charts.** I checked and updated the Gantt chart weekly, marking completed tasks and adjusting deadlines as needed.
- **Analyzing Changes.** I used updated visualizations to analyze the current state of the project and plan the next steps.

Using Visualizations for Motivation

Example from Personal Practice:
Visualization served as a powerful tool for maintaining motivation. I placed visual maps and charts in my workspace to constantly remind myself of my goals and the progress I had made.

Methodology:

- **Displaying Visualizations Prominently.** I hung the Gantt chart and flowcharts on the wall in my office so I could see them every day.
- **Tracking Progress.** Each time I completed a task, I marked it on the chart, which provided a sense of accomplishment and motivation to keep working.

Visualizing your plan is a powerful tool that helps you see the path to your goals clearly and follow it with confidence. By using tools like Gantt charts, flowcharts, and visual maps, you can effectively plan and manage the process of achieving your goals. Regularly updating and using visualizations for motivation will help you stay on track and achieve success.

6. Identifying Resources and Budget

Step 6: Identify Resources
When executing the plan, it's essential to consider all available resources and create a budget.
When you open an online store, you may need resources, such as funds for website development, salaries for employees, and marketing and advertising expenses.

Methodology:
- Make a List of Required Resources. Determine what resources you will need to execute the plan.
- Estimate the Budget. Calculate the costs for each resource and create a financial plan.
- Plan Resource Allocation. Determine how and when to use resources to achieve your goals.

7. Implementing and Managing Changes

Step 7: Manage Changes
During implementation, unexpected changes may arise and t's important to be flexible and adapt to these changes.
If you encounter technical difficulties while creating the website, you may need to revisit the plan or allocate additional resources to address the issues.

Methodology:
- Develop a Change Management Plan. Determine how you will respond to changes and what measures you will take.

- Adapt to New Conditions. Make adjustments to the plan and deadlines as needed.
- Communicate Changes to the Team. Ensure that all project participants are informed about the new plans.

8. Evaluation and Conclusion

Step 8: Conduct a Final Evaluation
After completing the plan, conduct a final evaluation. This will help you understand what went well and what can be improved.

Upon launching the online store, evaluate how successfully all subgoals and tasks were accomplished. Analyze what led to successful outcomes and what challenges arose.

Methodology:
- Gather All Data on Plan Execution. Assess the results for each subgoal and task.
- Conduct an Effectiveness Analysis. Identify which aspects of the plan were effective and what requires improvement.
- Develop an Improvement Plan. Use the insights gained to enhance future projects.

Creating a roadmap is a powerful tool that turns your dreams into reality. Clearly defining goals, breaking them into subgoals, creating a detailed action plan, and regularly monitoring progress will help you achieve success. Use visual tools, manage resources, and be prepared for changes. A final evaluation will allow you to improve your plans and reach even greater heights.

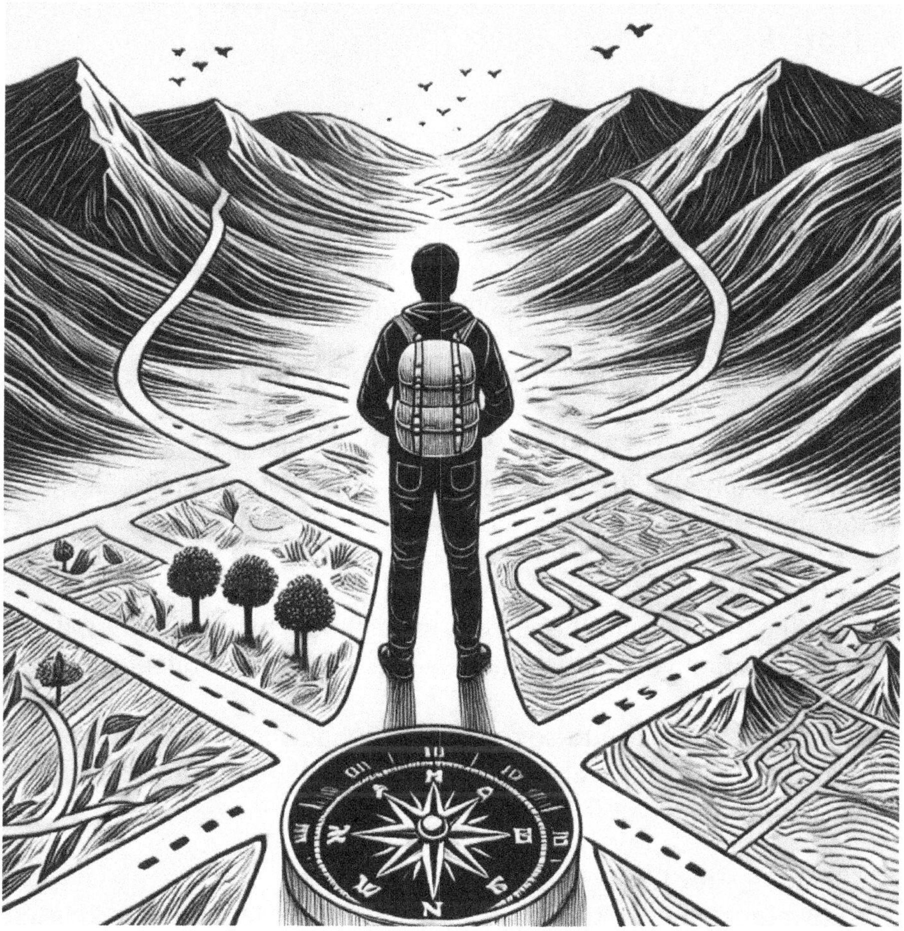

Chapter 5:
The Power of Habits

Habits are not just actions we perform daily; they shape our lives and can significantly change our path to success. In this chapter, we'll explore how small, consistent habits can play a crucial role in achieving your goals. We'll use examples from successful individuals to illustrate how to build productive habits and leverage them for great results.

The Habit of Waking Up Early: An Example from Tim Cook

Tim Cook, the CEO of Apple, is renowned for his habit of waking up early. He starts his day at 4:30 AM, giving him the advantage of a few quiet hours before the workday begins.

How It Works:
- Early Start: Cook uses the early morning hours to prepare for the day. This time without distractions allows him to focus on strategic planning and crucial tasks.
- Quiet Time: This period also provides the opportunity to read important reports, analyze results, and begin work on challenging projects without interruptions.

Methodology for Implementation:
- Set a Wake-Up Goal: Start by waking up 30 minutes earlier than usual. Gradually increase this time until you reach your desired result.
- Create a Morning Ritual: Define activities you will perform each morning. These could include exercise, meditation, or planning your day.
- Preparation: Use the morning hours to tackle tasks that require the most focus and energy.

Morning hours provide an advantage by allowing you to concentrate on important tasks and prepare for the upcoming day, ensuring greater productivity.

The Habit of Reading: An Example from Warren Buffett
Warren Buffett, one of the most successful investors in the world, places great importance on reading. He reads several hours daily, which helps him stay informed and make well-founded decisions.

How It Works:

- **Broad Perspective:** Buffett reads not only financial reports but also books on philosophy, history, and other fields, which helps him make more balanced decisions.
- **Consistency:** He has made reading a habit, allowing him to continually expand his knowledge and improve his investment strategies.

Methodology for Implementation:
- **Allocate Reading Time:** Schedule a specific time each day for reading. This could be in the morning, before bed, or during breaks.
- **Create a Reading List:** Compile a list of books and materials you want to read. This could include both professional literature and personal development books.
- **Take Notes:** While reading, jot down notes and ideas that could be useful in the future.

Regular reading helps broaden your perspective, improve knowledge, and make more informed decisions in your field.

The Habit of Physical Activity: An Example from Oprah Winfrey
Oprah Winfrey actively engages in physical activity, which helps her maintain both physical and mental health. She considers exercise an integral part of her life.

How It Works:
- **Energy and Vitality:** Regular exercise helps Winfrey maintain high energy levels and improves her mood.
- **Stress Resilience:** Physical activity aids in coping with stress and improves overall well-being.

Methodology for Implementation:
- **Choose an Activity:** Find a sport or exercise that you enjoy. This could be yoga, running, swimming, or strength training.
- **Create a Schedule:** Determine the time you will dedicate to workouts. This could be in the morning or evening, depending on your schedule.
- **Set Goals:** Establish specific objectives for your physical activity, such as improving endurance, losing weight, or increasing strength.

Regular physical exercise enhances both physical and mental health, contributing to an overall improvement in quality of life.

The Habit of Keeping a Journal: An Example from Richard Branson
Richard Branson, the founder of the Virgin Group, actively uses

journaling to record his thoughts and ideas. This habit helps him analyze his plans and assess progress.

How It Works:
- Awareness and Analysis: Writing in a journal helps Branson become aware of his ideas, challenges, and opportunities.
- Tracking Progress: A journal allows him to track his goals and observe how they materialize over time.

Methodology for Implementation:
- Record Thoughts and Ideas: Keep a journal where you write down your thoughts, ideas, and goals. Do this regularly to document your progress.
- Review Entries: Regularly revisit your entries to assess your achievements and adjust plans.
- Utilize Notes: Apply insights and conclusions from your journal in your work and personal life.

Journaling helps organize thoughts, plan actions, and track achievements.

The Habit of Networking: An Example from Mark Zuckerberg
Mark Zuckerberg, the founder of Facebook, actively engages in networking and expanding his network of contacts. This habit helps him discover new opportunities and ideas.

How It Works:
- **Network Development:** Zuckerberg actively engages with professionals in his field, which helps him find new ideas and opportunities.
- **Experience Exchange:** Networking allows for the exchange of experiences and knowledge with other successful individuals.

Methodology for Implementation:
- **Attend Events:** Regularly participate in events, conferences, and networking meetings related to your field.
- **Develop Contacts:** Strive to establish and maintain contact with people who can be beneficial for your development.
- **Exchange Ideas:** Take the opportunity to share ideas and experiences with other professionals. Active networking helps expand your professional contacts and find new opportunities.

The Habit of Self-Development: An Example from Bill Gates
Bill Gates, co-founder of Microsoft, dedicates time to self-development

and learning. He regularly studies new technologies and trends, which helps him stay at the forefront of his field.

How It Works:
- **Continuous Learning:** Gates consistently learns about new technologies and trends to remain competitive and implement innovations.
- **Application of Knowledge:** The knowledge gained is used to improve work and implement new ideas.

Methodology for Implementation:
- **Allocate Time for Learning:** Set aside time to learn new skills and knowledge, such as reading books, taking courses, or attending seminars.
- **Apply Knowledge:** Use the knowledge gained in your professional activities and life.
- **Regularly Update Skills:** Continuously monitor new trends and update your skills. Self-development helps you stay relevant, implement new ideas, and enhance your professional skills.

The Habit of Constant Self-Analysis: An Example from Steve Jobs
Steve Jobs, co-founder of Apple, was known for his practice of constant self-analysis. He regularly asked himself challenging questions and re-evaluated his approaches to work and life.

How It Works:
- **Progress Evaluation:** Jobs used self-analysis to assess his achievements and determine what needed to change.
- **Identifying Flaws:** Constant analysis helped him identify shortcomings and adjust his work methods.

Methodology for Implementation:
- **Regularly Ask Yourself Questions:** Take time to reflect on your goals and approaches. Ask yourself what can be improved.
- **Evaluate Your Results:** Periodically assess your achievements and analyze what works well and what needs adjustment.
- **Adjust Your Methods:** Use the insights gained to modify your methods and approaches.

I am proud to have developed the habit of waking up at 6 AM. This time has become a true gift for me, allowing me to start the day productively.

The first thing I do in the morning is exercise. By engaging in physical activity, I not only strengthen my body but also energize myself for the entire day. Exercise helps me feel alert and confident, and it boosts my mood. I notice that after my workout, tension dissipates, and clarity emerges in my thoughts.

After my workout, I dedicate time to reading literature. This not only broadens my horizons but also helps me find new ideas and inspiration. Reading makes me more open-minded and allows me to delve into various topics, contributing to my personal and professional growth.

These morning habits give me a sense of control over my day and boost my confidence. I see how they positively impact my productivity and overall well-being. Importantly, simple things like waking up early and exercising make my life more meaningful and fulfilling. I am happy that I have been able to develop these habits, and I intend to continue cultivating them so that each day is filled with opportunities and positive moments.

Chapter 6:
Overcoming Fear

Overcoming fear and doubt is a key step on the path to success. In this chapter, we will explore how to combat the internal barriers that hinder your progress and learn strategies to help you overcome the fear of failure. Using examples from successful individuals and personal experiences, we will discuss how to cope with these emotions and confidently pursue your goals.

Understanding Fear: From Within

Fear is a natural response of our body to uncertainty and potential threats. It can manifest in various forms, from the fear of failure to the fear of criticism. To effectively deal with fear, it is important to first understand what triggers it.

1. Identifying the Roots of Fear: Start by unraveling the roots of your fear. It may stem from fear of failure, fear of disapproval, or fear of the unknown. Try writing down your fears and analyzing them. For example, you may fear starting a new project because you worry it won't yield the expected results. Understanding this fear will help you determine its validity and how to confront it.

2. The Influence of Fear on Behavior: Fear can trigger various negative reactions, such as avoidance, procrastination, and self-doubt. It is essential to recognize how fear affects your behavior so that you can begin to act consciously.

Strategies for Overcoming Fear

1. The "Divide and Conquer" Method: This method involves breaking down a large fear into more manageable parts. Instead of focusing on the entire project at once, divide it into smaller tasks. For example, if you fear public speaking, start by preparing a short speech and practicing it in front of friends, gradually increasing the complexity. Elon Musk, founder of SpaceX, faced immense fears when his company was taking its first steps. Instead of being overwhelmed by the entire task of launching rockets, he focused on smaller parts of the process, such as testing and improving individual systems, which allowed him to overcome his overall fear and achieve success.

2. Cognitive Reprogramming Technique: This technique involves replacing negative thoughts with more constructive and positive ones. When you encounter negative thoughts like "I can't do this," replace them with more positive affirmations, such as "I am capable of overcoming challenges and achieving success."

Oprah Winfrey often faced self-doubt, especially in the early stages of her career. She used positive affirmations and self-encouragement to change her perspective and keep moving forward despite difficulties.

3. Gradual Exposure to Fear: Create a plan in which you gradually confront your fears. Start with smaller steps and gradually increase the difficulty. For instance, if you fear public speaking, start by speaking in front of a small group of friends and then progress to larger audiences.

J.K. Rowling, author of the Harry Potter series, overcame her fear of rejection by sending her manuscripts to publishers. Instead of stopping after the first rejections, she continued to submit her work, which eventually led to great success.

Working Through Internal Barriers
1. Visualization of Success: Imagine yourself successfully handling a task or overcoming a fear. Visualization can help strengthen your confidence and reduce anxiety.

Michael Jordan, the legendary basketball player, used visualization to prepare for games. He imagined himself successfully making key shots and winning matches. This practice helped him feel more confident in his actions on the court.

2. Creating an Action Plan: Develop a clear action plan that will help you deal with your fear. Include specific steps you will take to reduce fear and achieve your goals.

Ellen DeGeneres, a comedic actress and TV host, overcame her fear of a new project by creating a detailed action plan. This plan included researching the topic, working with experts, and regular rehearsals, which helped her approach new projects with confidence.

The Role of Support in Overcoming Fear
1. Surrounding Yourself with Supportive People: The first step is to recognize your fears. Try asking yourself questions: What exactly causes this fear? Why is it important to me? Writing down your thoughts will help you better understand your emotions and identify the roots of your fear.

Huge fears can seem overwhelming, so it's helpful to break them into smaller, manageable parts. For example, if you fear public speaking, start with small groups—first speaking in front of friends, then colleagues. Gradually increase the scale until you feel confident.

Negative thoughts often amplify fear. Instead of thinking, "I can't do this," try replacing that thought with, "I can do this." Positive affirmations will help you change your inner dialogue and boost your confidence.

The gradual exposure method can be very effective. Start with small steps and gradually increase the complexity of tasks. For example, if you fear talking to strangers, begin by simply smiling and saying hello. Then move on to short conversations, and later to longer discussions.

Visualization is a powerful tool. Imagine a situation that triggers fear, and picture yourself handling it successfully. Try to feel the positive emotions associated with achieving that result. This technique will help prepare you for real situations and reduce anxiety.

Support from friends, family, or colleagues can be crucial in overcoming fear. People who believe in you and support you can help you see opportunities and bolster your confidence. Don't hesitate to seek support. Talking to loved ones about your fears can significantly lighten the burden. Friends and family can offer helpful advice or simply support you in tough times. Support groups or connecting with like-minded individuals can also be very beneficial.

Fear is part of the journey of personal growth. Instead of viewing it as an obstacle, learn to use it as a means for development. By applying these strategies, you can not only overcome fears but also become a more confident person. Remember that every step, no matter how small, brings you closer to your goals. The path to overcoming fear can be challenging, but it is worth taking.

Brendon Burchard, an author and motivational speaker, shares how important the support of family and friends has been in his successful career. They helped him overcome fears and stay motivated.

2. Feedback and Mentorship: Receiving constructive feedback and working with mentors can help you address internal barriers and fears. Mentors can offer valuable advice and support during tough times.

Sheryl Sandberg, COO of Facebook, often spoke about the importance of mentorship and feedback from more experienced colleagues.

These recommendations helped her overcome fears and effectively lead the company.

Overcoming fear is not a one-time process, but rather an ongoing self-improvement effort. Fears can vary: fear of failure, social judgment, change, or even success. It is important to recognize that fear is a natural reaction and learn to manage it rather than avoid it. Here are several strategies that will help you confront internal barriers and confidently pursue your goals.

Chapter 7:
The Magnet of Motivation

In this chapter, we will delve into the art of maintaining high motivation despite obstacles and challenges. Motivation is an integral part of any successful journey, and by learning how to sustain it, you can overcome any hurdles and achieve your goals. We will explore various strategies and examples of successful individuals, as well as my personal experiences, to help you create your own motivation-maintaining system.

Understanding Sources of Motivation

Intrinsic and Extrinsic Motivation Motivation can be both intrinsic and extrinsic. Intrinsic motivation comes from your own desires and satisfaction from achieving goals, while extrinsic motivation may be linked to rewards, recognition, or approval from others.

Steve Jobs, co-founder of Apple, was driven by intrinsic motivation. His passion for innovation and desire to change the world of technology were more important than external rewards and recognition. This internal drive helped him overcome many challenges and build a successful company.

Identifying Personal Sources of Motivation
It is crucial to understand what specifically motivates you. This could be the desire to achieve a particular goal, the pursuit of self-improvement, or the wish to make a difference in the lives of others. Understanding your sources of motivation will help you create strategies to sustain them.

At the beginning of my journey as a designer, my motivation stemmed from a passionate desire to create something unique and valuable. It was essential for me to see my ideas come to life, and this internal drive supported me even in the toughest times.

Creating a Motivational Environment

Surrounding Yourself with Supportive People
Your environment plays a significant role in sustaining motivation. People who support, inspire, and believe in you can become an important source of energy and confidence.

Tony Robbins, a well-known motivational speaker, often emphasizes the importance of support from family and friends. His family encouraged him during tough times and helped him overcome doubts, which played a crucial role in his success.

Creating a Motivational Space
Create a physical space that inspires and supports your motivation. This could be a cozy workspace where you can focus on your goals or an area filled with inspiring quotes and items.

I designed my workspace to be as comfortable and inspiring as possible. I hung up photos of successful projects and achievements that reminded me of my goals and motivated me to move forward.

When I started my advertising agency, I broke down large goals into smaller tasks, such as finding clients, building a portfolio, and developing a team. Each achievement helped me maintain motivation and push forward.

Regular Self-Assessment and Plan Adjustment

Regularly Evaluating Progress
Assessing your progress regularly will help you stay on track. This allows you to see your achievements and make timely adjustments to your action plan.

Richard Branson, founder of the Virgin Group, regularly evaluates the success of his business projects and makes necessary adjustments. This adaptability allows him to respond to changing conditions and maintain high motivation.

Adjusting Plans and Goals
Be ready to make changes to your plans and goals as needed. Flexibility and adaptability are essential qualities for maintaining motivation and achieving success.

When my advertising agency faced financial difficulties, I revisited my goals and adapted my business plan. This helped me cope with challenges and continue moving towards success.

Using Motivational Tools

Visualization and Affirmations
Use visualization and affirmations to strengthen your motivation. Imagine

yourself achieving your goals and repeat positive statements to reinforce your confidence.

Lou Holtz, an American football coach, used visualization to prepare his players. He helped them envision themselves playing successfully, which boosted their confidence and motivation.

Motivational Books and Videos
Read motivational books and watch inspiring videos to gain new ideas and maintain a high level of motivation.

I read books and watched videos about motivation and personal growth, which helped me find new sources of inspiration and maintain high energy levels during difficult times.

Maintaining Work-Life Balance

Self-Care
Don't forget to take care of your physical and emotional health. A healthy lifestyle, balanced diet, and regular exercise will help you maintain high motivation and energy.

Oprah Winfrey places great importance on her health and well-being. She regularly exercises and practices meditation, which helps her maintain a high level of energy and motivation.

The Ability to Rest
Make time for rest and recovery. Breaks and downtime will help you avoid burnout and keep your motivation high.

I learned to allocate time for rest and recovery, which allowed me to maintain high productivity and motivation in the long run.

Conclusion
Maintaining motivation is not a one-time effort but a continuous process. By employing strategies such as understanding sources of motivation, creating a supportive environment, setting specific goals, regular self-assessment, utilizing motivational tools, and maintaining work-life balance, you can sustain high motivation and achieve your goals. By applying these principles and using examples from successful individuals, you can create your own system for maintaining motivation and moving toward success despite challenges and obstacles.

In my professional life, as in many others, there have been moments when fatigue and stress began to threaten my productivity and motivation. I realized that the key to long-term success and high efficiency lies not only in hard work but also in effectively managing my time for rest and recovery.

Recognizing the Issue

Early in my career, I often neglected the need for rest. I immersed myself in work, spending long hours at the computer and frequently losing track of time. This strategy seemed effective in the short term, but over time, I began to notice a decline in my productivity and an increase in stress. It became clear to me that without proper recovery, I could not maintain a high level of performance.

Creating a Rest Routine

Planning Regular Breaks

I implemented regular breaks into my work schedule. Every 90 minutes of work, I took a short break of 10-15 minutes. During these breaks, I would do light exercise, step outside for fresh air, or simply relax to give my eyes and brain a rest. These short breaks helped me maintain focus and avoid burnout.

Introducing Days Off

I used to work on weekends, but I realized it was important to set aside time for full rest. I began to plan my weekends to fully disconnect from work and dedicate time to family, hobbies, and relaxation. These weekends helped me recharge and return to work with new ideas and energy.

Caring for Physical Health

Taking care of my physical health became an important part of my routine. I started exercising regularly, which helped me relieve stress and maintain good shape. Additionally, I monitored my diet, choosing healthy foods that supported my energy levels and overall well-being.

Implementing Recovery Practices

Meditation and Mindfulness

I started practicing meditation and mindfulness, which helped me cope with stress and maintain calmness in high-pressure situations. Every morning, I dedicated 10-15 minutes to meditation, which allowed me to better manage my workload and keep a clear mind.

Hobbies and Interests
I carved out time for my hobbies, such as painting and traveling. These activities brought me joy and helped me take a break from work. They also stimulated my creativity and contributed to my personal growth.

Benefits and Results

Increased Productivity
After implementing regular breaks and days off, I noticed a significant improvement in my productivity. My ability to focus on tasks increased, and I was able to manage my time more effectively.

Reduced Stress
Regular rest and care for my physical health contributed to a decrease in stress levels. I became more resilient to work demands and recovered more quickly after challenging days.

Improved Quality of Work
With renewed energy and a fresh perspective on tasks, the quality of my work significantly improved. I became more creative and effective, positively impacting my project results.

Allocating time for rest and recovery became a key element of my professional success. It allowed me to maintain high productivity and motivation in the long term. By learning to manage my time effectively, I achieved sustainable success and avoided burnout, which is an important aspect of any professional endeavor.

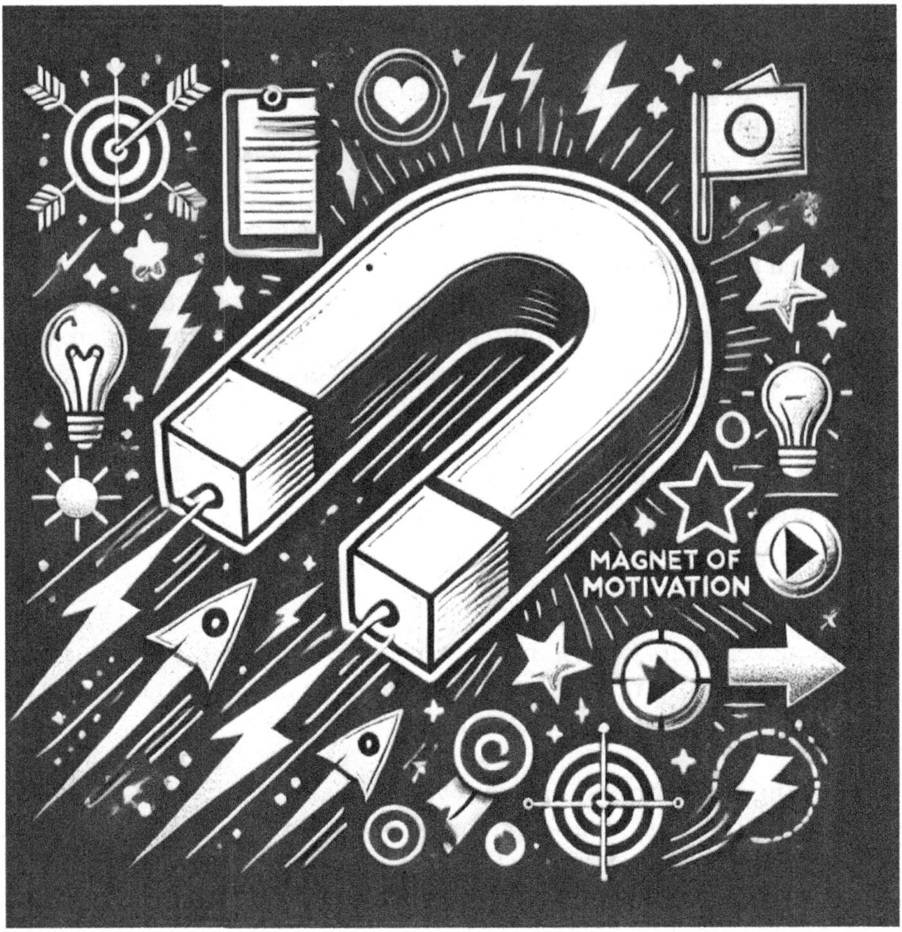
MAGNET OF
MOTIVATION

Chapter 8:
Masters of Time
How to Effectively Manage Time and Prioritize for Maximum Productivity

Learn to manage your time so that every action brings you closer to success.

Time management is key to success in any area of life. Effectively allocating your time not only helps you achieve your goals but also maintain balance among various aspects of your life. In this chapter, we will delve into the principles of time management so you can maximize your productivity and effectively reach your goals.

Understanding the Value of Time

Time as a Resource
Time is a unique resource that cannot be saved, stored, or regained. As Benjamin Franklin said, "Time is what we want most, but what we use worst." Recognizing the value of time will help you better manage your schedule and focus on important tasks. Time is money, but not only in a financial sense; it also encompasses your health, relationships, and happiness.

Time Analysis: Start by analyzing how you spend your time throughout the day. Record your activities and the time spent on them. This will help identify ineffective areas where your time can be better spent.

Priorities: Determine what is truly important to you. Prioritize based on how your actions affect your long-term goals and personal happiness.

The 80/20 Principle
The Pareto Principle, or the 80/20 rule, states that 80% of results come from 20% of efforts. This rule can help you focus on actions that yield the greatest benefits.

Identifying Key Tasks: Identify the 20% of tasks that deliver the most significant results. These may be actions directly related to your primary goals and projects.

Optimizing Efforts: Aim to minimize the time spent on less important tasks. For instance, if you spend a lot of time on emails, try reducing the frequency of checking your email or delegating that task to others.

Setting Goals and Priorities

Defining Goals
- **Specificity:** Formulate your goals to be clear and understandable. For example, instead of saying "I want to improve my skills," set a goal like "I want to complete a project management course by the end of the month.»
- **Measurability:** Ensure that you can track your progress towards your goal. For example, "Increase sales by 20% in the next quarter."

Eisenhower Principle

The Eisenhower Principle helps categorize tasks by urgency and importance:
- **Urgent and Important:** Tasks requiring immediate attention, such as resolving a work crisis.
- **Not Urgent, but Important:** Tasks that contribute to long-term goals, such as developing a strategy for a new project.
- **Urgent, but Not Important:** Tasks that can be delegated, such as administrative duties.
- **Not Urgent and Not Important:** Tasks that can be eliminated or postponed, such as unnecessary meetings.

Planning and Organization

Daily and Weekly Planning
Planning for the day and week helps create structure and organize your actions. This allows you to focus on the most important tasks and achieve your goals more effectively.
- **Daily Planning:** Create a plan for each day, allocating time for completing the most important tasks. Make sure to include time for breaks and rest.
- **Weekly Planning:** Develop an overarching plan for the week to see the big picture of your tasks and goals. This will help you coordinate various projects and prevent overload.

Using Tools
Modern technology can significantly simplify time management. Use tools and applications for planning and tracking tasks.
- **Trello and Asana:** These apps help organize tasks, prioritize them, and track progress. You can create boards and lists that make visualizing tasks easier.

• **Google Calendar:** Use it to plan meetings and reminders. Synchronizing with other devices will keep you informed and help you not miss important meetings.

Eliminating Distractions

Identifying Sources of Distraction
To manage your time effectively, it's essential to identify and minimize distractions. This may include notifications on your phone, social media, or noise in the office.
- **Analyzing Distractions:** Keep a record of what distracts you from work. This will help identify the most problematic sources of distraction.
- **Developing Strategies:** Take steps to eliminate these distractions. For example, set your phone to "Do Not Disturb" or use headphones to block out external noise.

Creating a Work Environment
The organization of your workspace plays a crucial role in productivity. A clean and organized space fosters concentration and reduces stress.
- **Organizing Your Desk:** Ensure that only necessary items are on your desk. Store unnecessary items in cabinets or drawers.
- **Creating a Comfortable Environment:** Ensure good lighting and a comfortable chair. This will help reduce physical strain and increase comfort levels.

Effective Project Management

Breaking Projects into Stages
Dividing large projects into smaller stages helps simplify management and track progress.
- **Task Decomposition:** Break the project down into several stages, each of which can be completed within a certain timeframe. This helps avoid overload and simplifies task execution.
- **Setting Deadlines:** Establish specific deadlines for each stage and adhere to them. This helps maintain the pace of work and prevents procrastination.

Delegating Tasks
Delegating tasks allows you to focus on the more critical aspects of the project while others handle less significant tasks.
- **Identifying Tasks for Delegation:** Determine which tasks can be assigned to other team members. These may include routine or less

critical tasks.
- **Communication and Trust:** Ensure clear communication about what is required from the person to whom you delegate a task. Trust your colleagues and allow them to perform the work.

Secrets of High Productivity

Pomodoro Technique
The Pomodoro Technique helps maintain focus and manage time more effectively by breaking work into short intervals.
- **Pomodoro Technique:** Work for 25 minutes, then take a 5-minute break. After four cycles, take a longer break of 15-30 minutes.
- **Benefits:** This method helps combat fatigue and maintain high productivity over extended periods.

Time for Inspiration
Setting aside time for reading and learning helps expand your horizons and discover new ideas for boosting productivity.
- **Reading and Learning:** Incorporate time into your schedule for reading books, articles, and attending training sessions. This will help you stay updated on new ideas and approaches.
- **Inspiration:** Seek inspiration from the stories of successful people and their approaches to time management. This can be an excellent source of motivation and new ideas.

Resilience and Self-Development

Reflection and Analysis
Regular reflection allows you to analyze your actions and improve your time management approaches.
- **Progress Analysis:** Periodically review your goals and achievements. Analyze what worked and what didn't, and make adjustments.

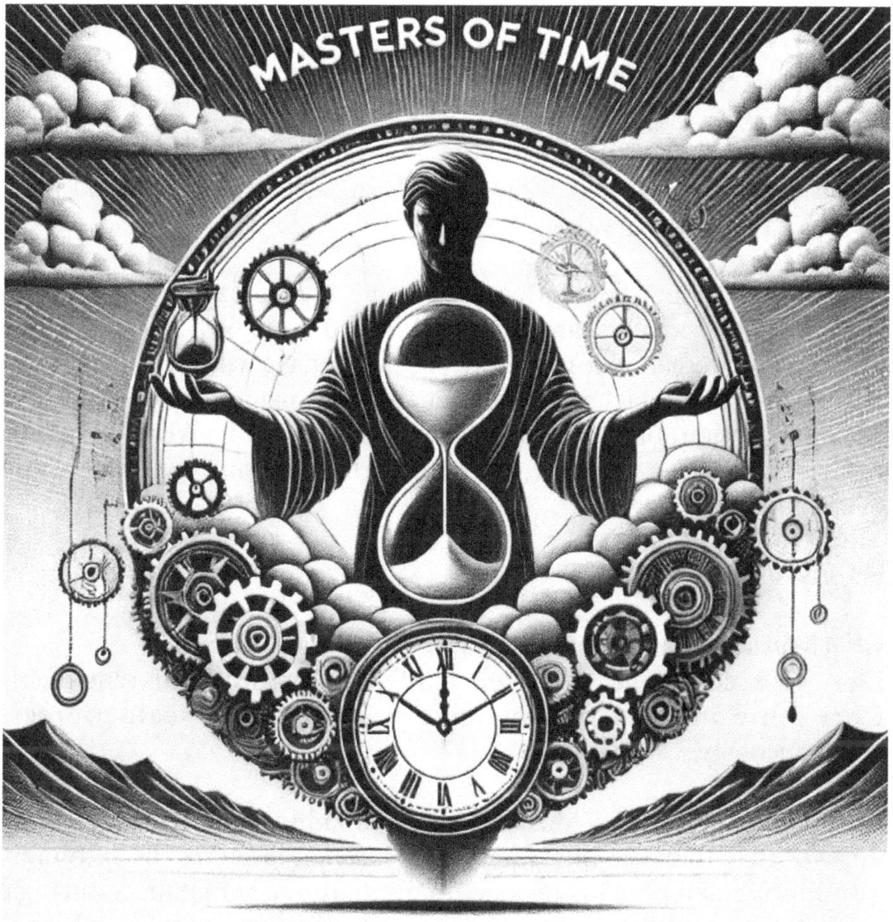
MASTERS OF TIME

Chapter 9:
Secrets of Successful People

Explore the habits and strategies of individuals who have achieved what you aspire to. Get inspired by the examples of successful people and adopt their best practices.

The journey to success is often winding and complex. However, many successful individuals share certain habits and strategies that have helped them achieve remarkable results. In this chapter, we will delve deeper into the habits and approaches that have enabled renowned figures to succeed and how you can apply these principles in your own life. We will examine their approaches to work, personal life, time management, and overcoming challenges.

Habits for Success

Elon Musk: Intense Work Ethic and Time Organization
Elon Musk, co-founder of SpaceX and Tesla, is known for his remarkable work ethic and ability to manage multiple large-scale projects simultaneously.

- 5-Minute Work Blocks: Musk employs a time-blocking method, dividing his workday into 5-minute intervals. This enables him to be extremely productive and plan his tasks with precision. For instance, during a workday, he might spend 5 minutes addressing a problem at SpaceX, then switch to discussing a new product for Tesla.
- Long-Term Projects: Musk focuses on major, long-term projects, such as colonizing Mars and transitioning to sustainable energy sources. This requires him to see the big picture and develop long-term strategies.
- Practical Example: When SpaceX was developing the Falcon 9 rockets, Musk personally engaged in technical details, allowing him to oversee the process and quickly respond to arising issues.

Oprah Winfrey: Morning Rituals and Positive Thinking
Oprah Winfrey, a media mogul and public figure, is known for her emphasis on personal development and morning rituals.

- Morning Rituals: Oprah starts her day with meditation, physical activity, and reading. This helps her stay focused and maintain a positive mindset. For example, her morning routine might include 20 minutes of meditation, followed by yoga and reading a book for inspiration.

- Personal Development: Winfrey dedicates significant time to personal development, attending seminars and reading books. She believes in the importance of lifelong learning and self-improvement.
- Practical Example: Winfrey actively works on expanding her knowledge in various fields, such as psychology and personal growth, using the insights she gains to inspire and educate others.

Strategies of Successful People

Jeff Bezos: "Working Backwards" Principle and Customer Focus

Jeff Bezos, founder of Amazon, employs a "working backwards" strategy which allows him to create long-term plans and effectively manage resources.

- Working Backwards: Bezos starts with the end goal and builds a plan from there. For example, if his goal is to create the best online marketplace, he begins by identifying customer needs and works backward to address those needs.
- Customer Focus: Amazon consistently places the customer at the center of its strategy. Bezos believes that understanding customer needs and continuously improving the user experience drives business growth.
- Practical Example: Amazon Prime was launched in response to customer demand for faster and more convenient service. This offering became one of the company's most successful products.

Jim Carrey: Visualization and Positive Thinking

Actor Jim Carrey is known for his practice of visualization and positive thinking, which have played a key role in his career.

- Visualization: Carrey wrote himself a check for $10 million for acting services and carried it with him. A few years later, he signed a contract close to that amount.
- Positive Thinking: Carrey believes in the power of positive thinking and visualization. He actively shares his experiences, inspiring others to believe in themselves and pursue their dreams.
- Practical Example: Carrey applied these principles while working on films such as "The Mask" and "Liar Liar." His approach helped him achieve outstanding results and gain recognition in the industry.

Developing Personal Habits
Tony Robbins: Goal Setting and Consistent Action

Tony Robbins, a renowned coach and author, advocates for setting clear goals and taking consistent actions to achieve them.

- Clear Goals: Robbins advises establishing specific and attainable goals to have a clear vision of what you want to achieve. For instance, instead of a vague goal like "I want to be successful," he recommends setting more specific goals, such as "Increase income by 20% in the next year."
- Consistent Action: Robbins emphasizes the importance of taking consistent action. Even small steps, if taken regularly, can lead to significant results.
- Practical Example: Robbins applies this approach in his training sessions, helping participants set specific goals and develop action plans to achieve them.

Richard Branson: Adventure and Embracing Risk
Richard Branson, founder of the Virgin Group, is known for his unconventional approach to business and life, which includes embracing risk and seeking new adventures.

- Embracing Risk: Branson is not afraid to take risks and challenge traditional business practices. He believes that risk is an essential element of innovation and growth. For example, he has expanded his business empire into unpredictable areas such as air travel and space tourism.
- Adventure as Motivation: Branson also uses adventure as a means to maintain motivation and inspiration. His passion for extreme sports, such as attempts to circumnavigate the globe in hot air balloons, serves as a source of energy and drive.
- Practical Example: When Branson launched Virgin Atlantic, he entered into a competitive battle with established airlines. His determination and willingness to take risks allowed Virgin Atlantic to carve out a niche in the market and become a successful player.

How to Apply Lessons from Successful People

Implementing Habits into Your Life
Adopt the habits of successful people to enhance your productivity and achieve your goals. Incorporate practices that you admire in those you look up to.

- Developing Rituals: Integrate morning rituals, such as meditation or physical activity, into your routine for increased productivity. For example, start your morning with 10 minutes of meditation and light exercise to set a positive tone for the day.
- Planning and Visualization: Utilize principles of visualization and backward planning to create strategies. Identify your end goals and

outline the steps needed to achieve them. Visualize how you will accomplish your goals and work through each step in your plan.

Continuous Learning and Development
Successful people constantly strive for learning and self-improvement. Foster growth and expand your knowledge by following their example.

- Reading and Learning: Regularly read books and attend training sessions to stay informed about new ideas and approaches. For example, set aside time each day to read books on personal growth or professional development.
- Seeking Inspiration: Look for inspiration in the stories of successful individuals and apply their methods in your own life. For instance, study the biographies of notable figures like Steve Jobs or Mary Kay Ash and adapt their strategies to your own goals.

Applying Principles and Methods
Don't just learn about the habits of successful people; apply their principles in your life. Continuously adapt your approaches and strategies based on what you've learned.

- Analysis and Adaptation: Analyze which habits and methods of successful people are most applicable to your situation. Implement them in your life and observe the results. For instance, if you notice that morning rituals help you be more productive, integrate them into your daily routine.
- Adjustment and Improvement: Periodically review your approaches and adjust them based on the outcomes and new insights. This will help you adapt to changes and continue to grow.

Studying and applying the habits of successful people can be the key to your own success. Get inspired by their methods, adapt their principles to your life, and watch how they help you achieve your goals. Remember that success does not come by itself—it requires consistent effort, learning, and adaptation. Use the lessons from successful people as a guide to create your own path to success and realize your dreams.

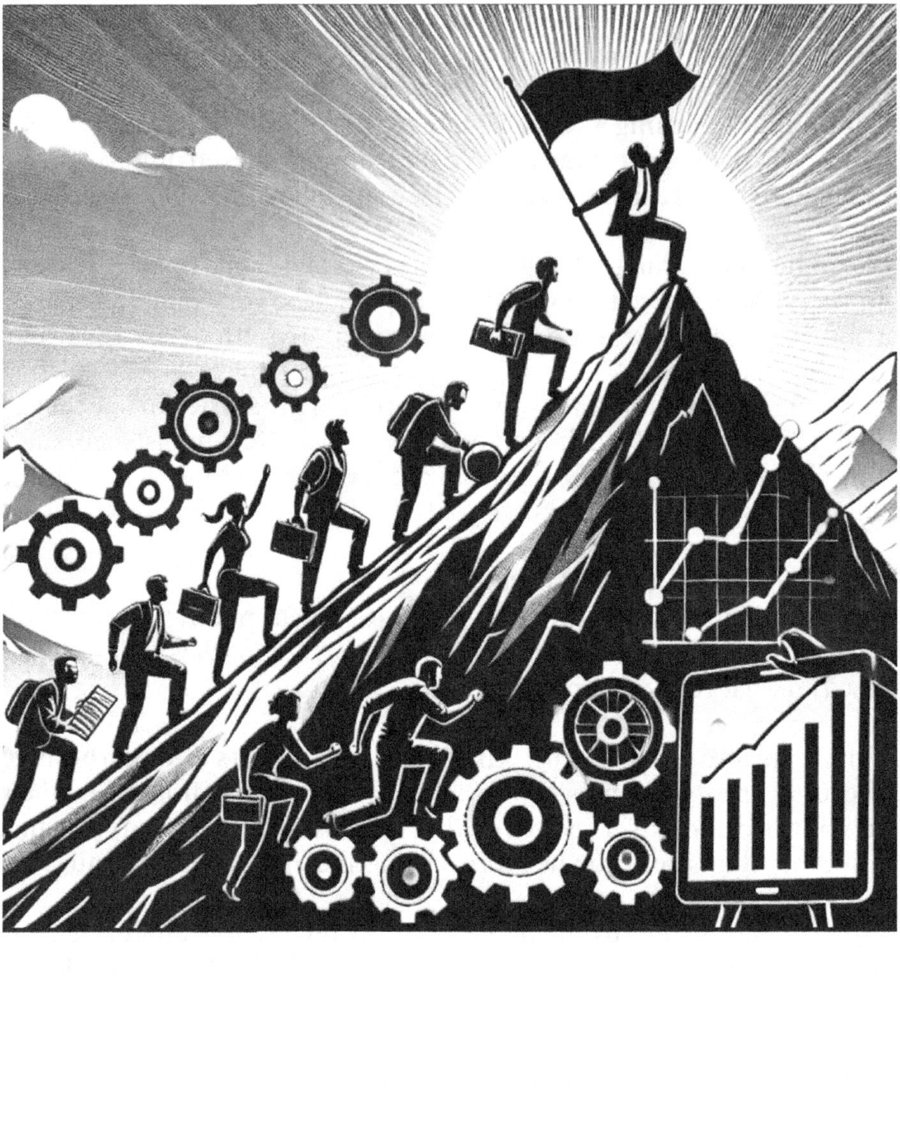

Chapter 10:
Transforming Failures

Failures, despite their unpleasant nature, are an essential part of the journey to success. They provide unique opportunities for personal growth and learning. In this chapter, we will explore how failures can be leveraged as a catalyst for achieving your goals and how the lessons learned can help you become more resilient and successful.

Embracing Failures as Part of the Journey
Failures do not define your ultimate outcome; rather, they shape your path to success. Accepting this fact helps maintain motivation and a positive attitude even in difficult times.

When my advertising agency went bankrupt, it was a significant blow. Instead of retreating, I realized that every mistake and challenge was part of the process. I began to view failures as necessary steps that contribute to my growth. This realization allowed me to maintain my determination and keep moving forward.

Example from Life: Steve Jobs
After being ousted from Apple in 1985, Steve Jobs could have chosen to retreat and abandon the business. However, he used this failure as an opportunity for a new beginning. He founded NeXT and later became one of the largest shareholders of Pixar. These ventures laid the groundwork for his return to Apple, where he led the company to new heights, including the creation of the iPhone and iPad. Steve Jobs used every failure as a lesson that helped him build successful businesses.

Analyzing Failures
Analyzing failures is key to understanding what went wrong and what can be improved. This involves identifying weaknesses, strategic missteps, and factors that contributed to the failure.

After my agency faced financial difficulties, I conducted a thorough analysis of the reasons behind our failure. I discovered that the main issue was an over-reliance on a single revenue source and insufficient attention to financial reserves. I also found that my marketing strategy was not flexible enough. This analysis helped me understand what needed to change to avoid repeating the same mistakes in the future.

Example from Life: James Dyson

James Dyson created over 5,000 prototypes of his vacuum cleaner before achieving commercial success. Each failed prototype provided him with new insights on what needed improvement. For instance, he learned that he needed to modify the filter design and airflow.
These lessons were invaluable in creating a successful bagless vacuum cleaner that revolutionized the industry.

Applying Lessons Learned
Applying lessons learned from failures involves developing new strategies and improving existing processes. This may require changing your approach to work, acquiring new skills, or revising your business model.

After overcoming financial difficulties, I invested in training and developing new skills. I studied best practices in financial management and devised new strategies for diversifying income. I implemented quality management and risk management systems that helped me create a sustainable business model. These changes enabled me to successfully relaunch the business and ensure its growth.

Example from Life: Oprah Winfrey
Oprah Winfrey faced numerous challenges throughout her career, including rejections from television producers and personal crises. Each of these challenges became a source of lessons and growth for her. She used these trials to improve her work, create new programs, and develop a unique style of communication with her audience. Oprah learned to adapt her strategy and leverage her failures as stepping stones to success.

The ability to adapt and change is what sets successful people apart. Each time you encounter a failure and learn from it, you build resilience. This quality allows you to better handle future challenges and becomes the foundation for achieving your goals. Resilience helps maintain motivation even when situations seem hopeless.

It is essential to change your perspective on failures: view them not as defeats but as opportunities for learning and growth. Each failure is a chance to enhance your skills and become stronger. Try to see them not just as obstacles but as valuable lessons leading you toward your goals.

Failures are not the end of the road; they are an important part of it. By applying strategies for analysis, extracting lessons, and adapting, you can transform your failures into sources of strength and inspiration. Every experience, even negative ones, can lead to new opportunities if you are willing to learn and change. Remember, your ability to overcome challenges and learn from failures defines your ultimate success. Believe in yourself and keep moving forward, as every step on this journey is a step toward your development.

Chapter 11:
The Power of Support

The support of those around us often becomes the key to success. It can determine how effectively you cope with difficulties and how quickly you achieve your goals. In this chapter, I will discuss how my environment influenced my journey, how I chose those who support me, and how this helped me achieve success. We will also highlight the importance of the right environment and provide examples from the lives of well-known individuals who benefited greatly from the support of their loved ones.

The Importance of Support on Your Journey
Support from others is not just comforting words; it is real help and faith in your abilities. When my advertising agency faced financial difficulties, it was particularly hard for me to cope with the pressure and stress. The feeling that my work could collapse weighed heavily on me. At that moment, the support of my family was critically important.

My wife, despite all the challenges, always stood by me. She was my reliable partner and source of strength. When I spent our last money to revive the business, she believed in me even when I began to doubt myself. Her words of encouragement and loyalty became the driving force that helped me move forward.

Example from Life: Elon Musk
Elon Musk, the founder of Tesla and SpaceX, also faced numerous challenges early in his career. When Tesla and SpaceX encountered financial troubles and product issues, his family and close friends provided emotional support and even financial assistance. His first business partner and other family members also had a significant impact on his ability to overcome difficulties.

How to Choose Supportive People
Choosing the right environment is an art. It is important to surround yourself with people who not only support you but also inspire you, provide constructive advice, and stand by you in tough times. I learned this from my own experience when selecting a team for my advertising agency after its relaunch.

When hiring employees, I focused on several key factors: their professional skills, values, and ability to work in a team. I sought those who were willing to invest their efforts in a common goal, who shared my vision, and who could offer fresh ideas. For example, I found a designer who, in addition to a high level of professionalism, had strong internal motivation and a positive attitude, which was crucial for creating a productive work environment.

Example from Life: Jack Ma
Jack Ma, the founder of Alibaba, also faced difficulties when building his company. He emphasized the importance of forming a team of people who shared his vision and determination. He brought on board individuals who were not only professionals in their fields but also willing to collaborate despite challenging conditions. These people helped him create one of the largest internet giants in the world.

How Support Can Become a Catalyst for Your Success
Support from those around you often acts as a catalyst for success, helping you overcome obstacles and realize your dreams. After assembling my team for my advertising agency, the support and belief of my colleagues became significant factors in the recovery and growth of the business.

Every successful project collaboration and every positive change we implemented was based on support and mutual assistance. My colleagues helped me analyze campaign results, find ways to improve, and develop new ideas. Their support and engagement made my agency competitive in the market, allowing us to acquire new clients and expand our operations.

Example from Life: Oprah Winfrey
Oprah Winfrey demonstrates how the support of others can become a catalyst for success. In the early stages of her career, her colleagues and mentors provided her with essential advice and support. This support allowed her to overcome numerous challenges and develop her career. Her success was largely made possible by being surrounded by people who helped her grow and evolve despite difficulties.

The influence of your environment on success cannot be overstated. The support of family, friends, and colleagues can be a decisive factor in achieving your goals. Our lives and careers largely depend on the people we spend time with and seek advice from. Our environment not only affects our mood but also shapes our views, behavior, and even ambitions.

It is important not only to seek such support but also to choose those who can genuinely help you grow and overcome difficulties. Just one word or gesture of support can inspire new achievements, while negative influences can significantly undermine your confidence. Therefore, it is crucial to carefully consider your surroundings.

My experience has shown that the right support and environment have been catalysts for my success. For instance, when I started a new project, I had people by my side who believed in me and supported me during tough times. Their advice and constructive criticism helped me refine my ideas and strategies, while their faith in me gave me the strength to continue when doubts arose.

Moreover, it is essential to remember that our environment shapes our outlook on possibilities. If you are surrounded by ambitious and goal-oriented people, this can be a powerful motivator for you. Interacting with successful and inspiring individuals broadens your horizons, helps you see new paths and opportunities that you might overlook alone. Such people can become not only sources of inspiration but also potential partners or mentors.

However, it is equally important to recognize that a negative environment can act as a brake on your path to success. If you are surrounded by people who do not believe in your goals or constantly criticize your aspirations, this can significantly diminish your motivation. They may intimidate you with failures and make you doubt your abilities. Therefore, it is vital to filter your surroundings and find those who genuinely support and inspire you.

Use the support of those around you as a resource to help you move toward your dreams and goals. Do not hesitate to share your ideas and ambitions with those who can provide constructive feedback. This not only helps refine your plans but also creates additional connections and opportunities for growth.

Remember, a strong environment is a powerful tool for achieving success. If you surround yourself with people who share your values and aspirations, it creates an atmosphere conducive to achieving your goals.

Your network can open doors you never imagined and provide opportunities that would be inaccessible alone.

It is also important to remember the value of mutual support. Strive to be as supportive and inspiring to others as you seek for them to be for you. Helping and caring for loved ones not only strengthens your relationships but also creates a positive environment that will support you on your path to success.

In conclusion, your environment plays a vital role in achieving success. Create a supportive and inspiring environment that will help you grow, develop, and achieve your goals. Remember that successful individuals do not act alone; they create a community around them ready to support and share their aspirations. Harness the power of your environment to turn your dreams into reality.

Chapter 12:
Plan B: When Things Don't Go as Planned

In life and business, things rarely go according to plan from start to finish. Unforeseen circumstances, market changes, or internal issues can derail even the most meticulously crafted strategies. In this chapter, I will discuss the importance of having a Plan B, how to adapt to changes, and how to respond flexibly to unexpected twists and turns. We will explore adaptation strategies, personal examples, and examples of successful individuals who effectively managed crises.

Why It's Important to Have a Plan B

A Plan B is not just a backup option; it is a strategic tool that helps maintain stability and confidence in unstable conditions. When my advertising business faced financial difficulties, I realized that it wasn't enough to have just one plan. I needed to be prepared for changes and have several backup strategies.

At the beginning of 2020, when the COVID-19 pandemic hit all industries, many companies found themselves in a difficult position. My business also faced serious challenges. Despite having well-thought-out strategies in place, it became clear that something more was needed to cope with the new reality.

Example from Life: Startups and the Pandemic

Many startups, especially in the restaurant and retail sectors, faced crises due to the pandemic. Those who had prepared a Plan B in advance were able to adapt more quickly. For example, many restaurants began offering delivery and takeout options, allowing them to survive during lockdowns.

How to Develop an Effective Plan B

To create an effective Plan B, several key aspects must be considered:

Risk Analysis

First, analyze potential risks and scenarios that could affect your plans. These could include financial difficulties, legislative changes, or even unexpected competition. I conducted a detailed analysis of possible risks for my business and developed several alternative strategies for different scenarios.

Creating Alternative Strategies

Based on the risk analysis, develop several alternative strategies. In my case, this included shifting focus to online marketing, reducing costs, and altering the business model. These alternatives enabled me to quickly adapt to the new conditions.

Resources and Support
Identify what resources and support you will need to implement Plan B. This could involve financial reserves, support from partners, or additional skills. In my situation, I brought in extra consultants and specialists to help adapt the business model to the new conditions.

Example from Life: Amazon and Expansion
When Amazon faced growing competition and market changes, the company developed several alternative strategies, including expanding its product range and developing cloud technologies. These steps allowed Amazon not only to survive but also to strengthen its market position.

Implementing Plan B and Adapting
When unforeseen circumstances arise, it's crucial to implement Plan B quickly and effectively. This requires not only good planning but also prompt action. In my case, when I needed to adapt the business model, I focused on the operational implementation of changes, such as adopting new technologies and optimizing processes.

Example from Life: Netflix and Business Model Change
Netflix initially started as a DVD rental service, but with the development of technology and changes in consumer preferences, the company transitioned to streaming video. This shift was part of a Plan B that allowed Netflix to become a leader in the streaming industry.

Evaluation and Adjustment
After implementing Plan B, it's important to evaluate its effectiveness and make adjustments as needed. In my case, after implementing changes, I regularly analyzed the results and adjusted the strategy to achieve maximum effectiveness.

Example from Life: Apple and Product Strategy
When Apple faced challenges in the smartphone market, the company reevaluated its product strategy and began actively developing new technologies such as virtual reality and enhanced camera features. This enabled Apple to adapt to changing conditions and maintain its competitiveness.

Conclusion

Plan B is not just a backup option; it is a crucial element of risk management strategy and adaptation to change. In today's fast-paced and unpredictable world, having a clear action plan for unforeseen circumstances is essential. If you are prepared for various scenarios, it not only mitigates the impact of setbacks but also allows you to adapt more quickly to new conditions.

Having a Plan B makes you feel more confident in your actions. This sense of confidence allows you to focus on your goals and keep moving forward, even when obstacles arise. My experience has shown that flexibility and readiness for change are key factors in overcoming crises and achieving success. When your initial plan fails, it's vital not to panic but instead to turn to the alternative strategies you have prepared in advance. This not only reduces stress but also helps maintain focus on important tasks.

Additionally, developing a Plan B fosters a deeper understanding of your goals and resources. The planning process involves analyzing potential risks and assessing what might go wrong. This helps you better understand what actions need to be taken in a difficult situation and what resources you may need. Such an approach allows you to identify weaknesses in your initial plan and improve it, ultimately making you better prepared for unexpected twists.

Using Plan B also enhances your problem-solving skills. When you face obstacles, the ability to quickly adapt and find alternative routes to your goals becomes an invaluable asset. It builds your confidence in your abilities and enhances your capacity to tackle new challenges. It's important to remember that setbacks are not the end, but rather opportunities for learning and growth. A flexible approach allows you to learn from failures and apply those lessons for further development.

Moreover, having a backup plan helps you manage resources effectively. When you've thought through various courses of action in advance, you can allocate your time and resources optimally, significantly increasing your chances of success. This also helps prevent burnout that can arise from relentless attempts to achieve results when the initial plan isn't working.

Equally important, Plan B helps you stay connected with your team and your environment. When you share your alternative strategies with others, it fosters an atmosphere of trust and support. People are more willing to help if they know you have a clear plan of action in case of problems. In this way, you not only strengthen your position but also create strong connections that can be crucial in tough times.

In conclusion, preparation for unexpected turns and the ability to adapt are key components of successful progress toward your goals. Use this approach to maintain confidence and effectiveness on your path to success. Remember that having a Plan B is not a sign of weakness, but a demonstration of wisdom and strategic thinking. It enables you to move forward with greater assurance, knowing that even if something goes wrong, you are prepared to handle it and navigate any challenges. Your ability to adapt and find solutions to difficult situations defines your success and helps you realize your dreams.

Chapter 13:
Time-Outs for Reflection

In today's fast-paced world, where change is constant and demands for efficiency are high, it is essential not only to take action but also to pause regularly and assess our journey. Time-outs for reflection allow us to evaluate our achievements, analyze mistakes, and adjust our strategies. In this chapter, we will explore the importance of conducting regular self-assessments, how to do it effectively, and the benefits it can bring.

The Importance of Time-Outs for Reflection
Time-outs for reflection are moments when we stop to evaluate current results, analyze our actions, and contemplate the future. This time for self-analysis helps us understand what works, what doesn't, and what corrections need to be made.

Personal Experience: Periodic Business Assessments
When I managed my advertising agency, I regularly set aside time to analyze achieved results. Every three months, I conducted a review of key performance indicators, assessed successes and failures, and adjusted the business strategy based on this analysis. This allowed me to adapt to market changes and improve business processes.

How Regular Reflection Helps Regular reflection offers numerous advantages: Assessing Achievements and Progress

It helps us understand how far we've come in reaching our goals. It also aids in identifying which steps have been most successful and which strategies need modification.

Identifying Mistakes and Problems
Regular reflection helps pinpoint mistakes and issues that may have arisen during the process. This gives us the opportunity to rectify them before they become significant obstacles to success.

Adjusting Strategies
Reflection allows us to adapt our strategies and action plans in accordance with changes in the external environment or internal factors. This ensures flexibility and the ability to respond to new challenges.

Historical Example: Corporate Reflection at IBM
In the 1990s, when IBM faced a downturn, the company undertook a

comprehensive reflection of its strategy and business model. This enabled IBM to focus on new technologies and services, such as cloud computing and data analytics, which facilitated a successful recovery and growth.

How to Conduct Effective Reflection

To make reflection beneficial, it's crucial to approach the process correctly: Establish Regular Intervals

Determine the frequency with which you will conduct self-assessment. This can be a monthly, quarterly, or annual review, depending on your goals and needs.

Use Specific Metrics
Identify key performance indicators (KPIs) that will serve as the foundation for evaluating your achievements. These can include financial metrics, performance indicators, or any other measurements important for your success.

Analyze and Draw Conclusions
During the analysis, focus not only on results but also on the processes that led to them. Identify what worked well and what requires improvement.

Personal Experience: Periodic Project Audits
In my advertising agency, I applied the methodology of periodic audits for all projects. This included gathering feedback from clients, analyzing campaign results, and assessing the internal effectiveness of the team. This approach allowed me to identify issues promptly and optimize operations.

Benefits of Regular Reflection
Regular reflection yields the following advantages: Improved Efficiency

It helps to identify weaknesses and enhance processes, leading to an overall increase in work efficiency.

Increased Motivation
Seeing your achievements and progress provides additional motivation for further development and reaching new goals.

Adaptation to Changes
Regular assessment allows for timely adaptation to changes and adjustments of strategies according to current realities.

Real-Life Example:
Starbucks and Reflection Starbucks regularly conducts internal reviews and assessments of its strategy, enabling the company to adapt to market changes and consumer preferences. This practice has helped Starbucks maintain its leadership in the coffee shop industry.

Practical Steps for Implementing Time-Outs
To effectively implement time-outs for reflection, follow these steps:
Schedule Reflection Time

Determine a specific time in your schedule for conducting self-assessment. This could be at the end of the week or month.

Prepare Materials
Gather all necessary data and materials for analysis. These may include reports, statistics, feedback, and other important documents.

Analyze and Discuss
Conduct an analysis of the data gathered and discuss the results with your team or a mentor. Develop an action plan based on the insights gained.

Implement Changes
Based on the analysis conducted, make necessary adjustments to your strategy or action plan. Ensure that the changes are reflected in your work processes.

Personal Experience: Reviewing and Adjusting Business Plans
Every quarter, I reviewed my business plans and made necessary changes based on current results and market conditions. This allowed me to keep the strategy relevant and adapt to changing circumstances.

Conclusion
Time-outs for reflection are a key element of successful management and goal achievement. In a modern world where the pace of life is rapid and demands are constantly increasing, it is crucial to find time for pauses and contemplation. These time-outs not only allow us to evaluate our achievements but also to adjust our actions to ensure we are moving in the right direction.

Often, we become immersed in daily tasks, forgetting to stop and ask ourselves: am I truly moving toward my goals? Reflection helps us see the bigger picture and identify details that may escape our attention in the routine.

Regular self-assessment enhances efficiency, boosts motivation, and enables adaptation to changes. It serves as an internal audit that allows us to analyze what works and what doesn't. It is important to ask ourselves key questions: what successes have I achieved recently? What challenges have I faced, and how did I handle them? What skills or knowledge do I need to develop to improve results? This analysis not only helps us recognize our achievements but also understand what needs to be changed to reach even greater heights.

Moreover, time-outs for reflection create space for creative thinking. When we step away from the daily hustle, we gain the opportunity to view the situation from a different angle. This can lead to new ideas and approaches that we might not have noticed in a typical environment. Often, the most valuable insights come precisely when we allow ourselves to think and ponder our thoughts and feelings.

Using this approach also helps maintain a balance between professional and personal life. It is important to remember that successful time and goal management is not solely about work. Time-outs for reflection allow us to evaluate how our work impacts our overall life and take measures to improve this balance. This can be especially beneficial when work becomes a source of stress or burnout.

Additionally, regular reflection strengthens our ability to adapt to changes. In a rapidly changing world, it is essential to be prepared for new challenges and circumstances. Time-outs enable us to stay connected to our goals and values, even when external conditions shift. This helps maintain focus and not lose sight of what truly matters.

Another important aspect is that reflection fosters the development of self-improvement skills. By analyzing our actions and results, we can identify areas where we want to grow. This not only helps us become more qualified professionals but also creates a sense of progress and achievement. Each step toward self-improvement bolsters our confidence and motivation.

Ultimately, time-outs for reflection are a powerful tool for enhancing productivity and achieving success. Use this approach to make your work more effective and successful while maintaining flexibility and the ability to improve. Remember that successful people are those who can not only act but also reflect on their actions. Pausing for thought can be the key that unlocks doors to new opportunities and accomplishments.

By investing time in reflection, you lay the groundwork for future successes and professional growth.

Chapter 14:
Actions and Reactions

In a world full of uncertainty and change, a proactive approach is key to creating opportunities and achieving success. In this chapter, we will explore how proactive actions can open new horizons, how to leverage your actions to create opportunities, and how proactive behavior influences success.

Understanding the Proactive Approach
Proactivity is the ability to take independent action, anticipating the future and taking measures to shape it rather than merely reacting to what happens. A proactive approach includes:

Taking Responsibility
Instead of blaming external circumstances, proactive individuals take responsibility for their actions and their consequences.

Initiative
Proactive people do not wait for something to happen; they create opportunities themselves and actively engage in problem-solving.

Planning
A proactive approach involves long-term planning and anticipating potential challenges, as well as developing strategies to overcome them.

Personal Experience: Overcoming Financial Difficulties
When I faced financial difficulties in my advertising agency, I didn't just wait for the situation to improve. Instead, I actively sought out new sources of income, revamped the business model, and found alternative ways to attract clients. These actions helped me not only to overcome the crisis but also to strengthen the business.

By adopting a proactive mindset, we position ourselves to seize opportunities, adapt to changes, and ultimately succeed in an ever-evolving environment.

How Proactive Actions Create Opportunities

Proactive actions open up a multitude of opportunities:
•1. Creating New Projects and Ideas
Proactive individuals don't wait for new opportunities to arise; they

initiate projects and ideas that can lead to success.

•2. Overcoming Obstacles
Instead of facing obstacles and waiting for them to disappear, proactive people seek ways to overcome them and solve emerging problems.

3. Building Networks
Proactivity also involves establishing and strengthening connections with others, which can open new possibilities for collaboration and partnerships.

Example from History: James Dyson, the creator of Dyson, invented his revolutionary vacuum cleaner after becoming frustrated with traditional models. He demonstrated proactivity by developing a new solution, ultimately achieving global success after many years.

Strategies for Proactive Behavior

To effectively utilize a proactive approach, follow these strategies:

1. Define Goals and Priorities
Clearly outline your goals and priorities. This will help direct your actions and create opportunities that align with your ambitions.

2. Develop an Action Plan
Create an action plan that includes steps to achieve your goals and overcome potential obstacles. This will help you stay organized and proactive.

3. Seek Opportunities for Growth
Continuously look for opportunities for growth and development. This may include new projects, additional training, or expanding your network of contacts.

Example from Personal Experience:
When I decided to expand my advertising agency, I developed a strategic plan that included launching new services and implementing advanced technologies. This proactive approach allowed me to strengthen my business and attract more clients.

Example from Personal Experience: A Proactive Approach to a Crisis in My Advertising Agency
When I faced a financial crisis in my advertising agency, I found myself confronted with the challenging task of overcoming difficulties and finding new paths for growth.

This experience became a lesson in proactive approaches for me, demonstrating how active actions can create new opportunities and help navigate challenging situations.

Step 1: Accepting Reality and Assessing the Situation
The first steps I took included a honest evaluation of the current situation. I realized that, although the crisis was serious, it did not define my future success. Taking responsibility for the current state of the business was a pivotal moment. Instead of looking for reasons outside the company, I focused on what I could do myself to improve the situation.

Analyzing Financial Condition: I conducted a detailed analysis of the company's financial condition to understand which aspects of the business model needed to change.

Assessing the Market and Competition: I studied the market and competitive landscape to understand what changes had occurred and how they were affecting my business.

Step 2: Developing New Strategies
After assessing the situation, I began developing new strategies to help overcome the crisis. In this process, I applied a proactive approach, which included the following actions:

Redesigning the Business Model: I reviewed the agency's business model and identified opportunities for optimization. This included reducing costs, streamlining internal processes, and seeking new revenue sources.

Searching for New Clients and Projects: I actively sought new projects and clients. To do this, I employed various marketing strategies, such as participating in networking events, enhancing social media presence, and developing partnerships.

Investing in Training and Development: I invested in training for my team to enhance their skills and broaden their capabilities. This allowed us to offer new services and improve the quality of our work.

Step 3: Implementing the Plan and Adjusting Actions
Once I had developed new strategies, I began implementing them. This process was dynamic and required flexibility:

Implementing Changes: I introduced changes in business processes that reduced costs and increased the efficiency of the agency's operations.

Regular Monitoring of Results: I regularly tracked the results of the implemented changes and adjusted actions based on their effectiveness. This approach helped me respond quickly to emerging problems and make necessary adjustments.

Feedback from the Team: I actively gathered feedback from my team and considered their suggestions. This helped me better understand employee needs and improve internal processes.

Step 4: Evaluating Results and Planning for the Future
As we began to overcome the crisis, I focused on evaluating results and developing future plans:

Analyzing Achievements: I analyzed my results to understand which strategies were most effective.

Long-term Development Planning: I developed a long-term growth plan that included new goals, projects, and initiatives.

Strengthening Partnerships: I continued to develop and strengthen partnerships, allowing us to expand our client base and improve financial performance.

The proactive approach I applied during the financial crisis demonstrated how active actions can create new opportunities and help overcome challenges. An honest assessment of the situation, the development of new strategies, flexibility in implementing plans, and constant monitoring of results became key elements of my success. This experience taught me that proactivity helps address current issues as well as opening new horizons for future development.

Overcoming Common Mistakes in a Proactive Approach
Many face difficulties trying to be proactive. Here are some common mistakes and ways to avoid them:

Avoiding Risk: Some people shy away from proactivity due to fear of risk. It's important to learn how to manage risks and see them as opportunities for growth.

Lack of Planning: Proactivity requires clear planning. Uncertainty and lack of a plan can lead to inefficiency.

Ignoring Feedback: Proactivity does not mean ignoring the opinions of others. It is essential to consider feedback and adjust actions as needed.

Historical Example: Elon Musk

Elon Musk, the founder of SpaceX and Tesla, faced numerous challenges and failures on his path to success. However, his proactive approach to problem-solving and willingness to take risks enabled him to overcome these challenges and achieve significant accomplishments.

Real-Life Examples of Proactive Approaches

1. Richard Branson and Virgin: Richard Branson demonstrated proactivity by starting businesses in various industries despite the risks. He founded Virgin Records and then expanded into aviation and space industries, creating opportunities and overcoming obstacles.

2. Oprah Winfrey and Her Media Empire: Oprah Winfrey exhibited proactivity by starting her career as a television host and developing her own media resources. Her initiative and ability to create opportunities led to a successful media empire.

3. Jeff Bezos and Amazon: Jeff Bezos utilized a proactive approach by starting with an online bookstore and eventually creating one of the largest retail platforms in the world. His proactive actions and foresight contributed to the creation of vast opportunities.

Conclusion

A proactive approach is key to creating opportunities and achieving success. It is not just the ability to react to events but an active stance based on taking responsibility for one's life and actions. Proactive individuals do not wait for opportunities to appear; they seek them out and create conditions for growth and development. This approach involves initiative, planning, and a willingness to change.

Use a proactive approach in your life and career to create opportunities, overcome obstacles, and move toward success. We can all learn from these examples and start applying proactivity in our daily lives. Ask yourself: How can I improve my current situation?

What opportunities can I create for myself and others? Start small—define your goals and develop an action plan. Each step in this direction strengthens your confidence and opens new horizons.

Proactivity also implies a readiness for change. In a world where nothing stands still, the ability to adapt and seek new paths becomes especially important. Be open to learning and new ideas, and don't be afraid to step outside your comfort zone. Strive to surround yourself with people who share your ambitions and inspire you to take action. Your support network can significantly influence your achievements.

Remember, a proactive approach is not just a strategy; it's a way of life. It's about being ready not to wait for something to happen but to take action on your own. Proactivity allows you to achieve your goals and create a positive impact on those around you. Harness this power to become the architect of your destiny and move forward, regardless of the circumstances.

Chapter 15:
The Magic of Small Things

In a world of big ambitions and grand plans, it's easy to forget that small steps and details can play a crucial role in achieving significant goals. This chapter is dedicated to the importance of the little things on your journey to success. We will explore how attention to detail and small actions can profoundly impact your success and provide examples from the lives of successful individuals who have harnessed the "magic of small things" to achieve their goals.

Introduction to the Magic of Small Things

Small things are those little yet significant elements that often go unnoticed. Externally, they may seem inconsequential, but their impact on the overall outcome can be enormous. This principle applies to any endeavor, whether in business, personal growth, or everyday tasks. Paying attention to the little things not only helps avoid mistakes but also creates the conditions for achieving outstanding results.

Principles of the Magic of Small Things

1. Consistency and Regularity: Consistent small steps often lead to significant results. This can involve daily completion of minor tasks, continuous self-improvement, or maintaining discipline in work.

Example from Life: Thomas Edison, the inventor of the light bulb, is known for his method of trial and error. He didn't stop when he faced setbacks; his persistence and attention to detail allowed him to make breakthroughs in electric lighting despite numerous small failures.

2. Focus on Quality: Paying attention to quality, even in minor aspects of work, can significantly improve the outcome. This can involve accuracy in task execution, careful planning, or attention to detail in a project.

Example from Life: Steve Jobs, co-founder of Apple, paid great attention to detail in the design of his products. He believed that every element, even those not visible to users, should be of the highest quality. This attention to detail helped create products that became benchmarks for quality and innovation.

3. Personal Approach: Small details often relate to a personal approach. By knowing your goals and tasks, you can tailor your work to account for specific little things that will matter to you.

Example from Life: Oprah Winfrey, media personality and entrepreneur, paid attention to the little things in her work and life. She sought to create a unique and personal experience for her audience, which allowed her to gain immense popularity and recognition.

How Small Steps Impact Big Goals

1. Gradual Achievement of Goals: Big goals are often achieved through the completion of small but significant steps. These steps may seem insignificant, but their regular execution contributes to progress.

Example from Life: J.K. Rowling, author of the Harry Potter series, spent many years writing and editing her book. Each day, she took small steps toward completing her work, which ultimately led to the creation of one of the most successful literary projects of modern times.

2. Turning Mistakes into Lessons: Paying attention to small things helps avoid major mistakes and allows one to learn from failures. This fosters personal and professional growth.

Example from Life: Michael Jordan, one of the greatest basketball players of all time, faced numerous failures on his path to success. However, he used his mistakes as opportunities for growth, focusing on the details in his training and strategy, which allowed him to become a leader in his sport.

Mistakes and failures are inevitable parts of any path to success. However, instead of viewing them as obstacles, successful individuals see them as opportunities for growth and learning. In this chapter, we will explore how to transform mistakes into powerful lessons that will help you become more resilient and goal-oriented.

Embracing Mistakes

1. Acknowledgment of Failures: The first step in turning mistakes into lessons is acknowledging them. It's essential to honestly assess your actions, understand what went wrong, and take responsibility for your errors. This helps avoid denial and allows you to consciously work on rectifying the situation.

Example: John Snow, a popular entrepreneur in the technology sector, faced a major setback when his first startup failed due to poor financial management. Instead of giving up on his ambitions, he acknowledged his mistakes and used that experience to build a more successful business in the future.

2. Understanding the Causes: It's crucial to delve into the reasons that led to the mistakes. This helps to identify what specifically caused the failure and which factors can be improved. Understanding the root causes of errors is key to preventing their recurrence.

Example: Elon Musk encountered problems when launching SpaceX's first rockets. He and his team meticulously analyzed every aspect of the launch, including rocket designs and assembly processes, to determine what went wrong. This analysis significantly improved their technology and led to success in subsequent missions.

Using Mistakes for Reflection

1. Analysis and Reflection: After acknowledging and analyzing mistakes, it's important to conduct deep reflection. Assess how the mistake impacted your work and you personally. Consider what lessons can be learned and how to apply this knowledge in the future.

Example: J.K. Rowling, author of the Harry Potter series, faced rejections from publishers early in her career. Instead of despairing, she used that experience to refine her writing skills and deepen her understanding of the book market, ultimately leading to the international success of her books.

2. Adopting a New Perspective: Mistakes often open up new perspectives and opportunities. Failures can provide unique insights and ideas that might have gone unnoticed without the errors.

Example: Walt Disney faced failures with several projects before creating Disneyland. His setbacks helped him understand what was needed to create a successful amusement park and allowed him to integrate innovative ideas that made Disneyland a global phenomenon.

Applying Lessons from Mistakes

1. Implementing Changes: Apply the lessons learned to future projects and actions. Use the knowledge gained to adjust your strategies, improve processes, and make more informed decisions.

Example: Oprah Winfrey, after experiencing failures in television and radio, created a unique show format that was more personalized and audience-oriented. Her ability to learn from her mistakes led to the establishment of a successful media platform and strengthened her image as a leading interviewer.

2. Developing Resilience: Overcoming failures fosters the development of resilience. Each time you face difficulties, you become more steadfast and prepared for new challenges.

Example: Michael Jordan, a renowned basketball player, was cut from his high school basketball team, but this only fueled his determination to become the best player. He continued to work on his skills and became one of the greatest players in basketball history.

Practical Steps for Turning Mistakes into Lessons

1. Create a Mistake Journal: Record your mistakes, analyze their causes, and document the lessons learned. This will help you organize your knowledge and avoid repeating the same mistakes in the future.

2. Discuss Mistakes with a Mentor: Share your mistakes and lessons with an experienced mentor or colleague.

Discussing problems and solutions with an outside person can provide new perspectives and ideas.

3. Develop an Action Plan: Based on the lessons learned, create an action plan that will help you avoid repeating mistakes and improve your approaches.

4. Regularly Review: Periodically revisit your records of mistakes and lessons to remind yourself of what you have learned and apply that knowledge to your current activities.

Mistakes are not the end of the road but an important stage on the path to success. Many people fear making mistakes, viewing each failure as a serious setback. However, it is often the mistakes and failures that provide the most valuable lessons in our lives. They open our eyes to our weaknesses and shortcomings, allowing us to understand what needs to be improved to move forward. Turning mistakes into lessons helps you grow and develop, providing new opportunities for improvement and achieving your goals. Instead of blaming yourself for mistakes, it's crucial to focus on what you can learn from them.

Mistakes give us a unique opportunity to analyze our actions and assess what exactly went wrong. For instance, if you encounter a failure in project mistakes - In a project, it's essential to ask yourself questions like: What decisions were made incorrectly? What could have been done differently? This analytical process not only helps you understand where you went wrong but also allows you to develop a strategy for future actions. Utilizing mistakes as a tool for learning and adaptation enables you to avoid repeating the same missteps, thereby improving your chances of success in the future.

It's also important to remember that mistakes do not make you less competent or less successful. On the contrary, they signify that you are trying new things and stepping outside your comfort zone. Every successful person has faced failures along their journey. For instance, many well-known entrepreneurs and leaders, such as Richard Branson and Oprah Winfrey, acknowledge that their successes are largely based on the lessons they learned from their mistakes. Their stories demonstrate that perseverance and the ability to adapt are key factors on the road to success.

Additionally, mistakes can help you become more confident in your actions. When you learn to cope with failures and find positive aspects in them, you become more resilient. This confidence allows you to move forward, even when challenges arise. Each time you overcome an obstacle, your sense of confidence grows, and you start to view mistakes as a part of the process rather than a final verdict.

It is also crucial to share your mistakes with others. Openness about your missteps can strengthen connections with those around you and create an atmosphere of trust. You may help others avoid the same mistakes, which can be particularly beneficial in teams or workplaces. This fosters a culture where mistakes are seen as part of the learning process rather than something negative. As a result, not only do you develop your own skills, but you also contribute to the growth of others.

In conclusion, mistakes are not obstacles but opportunities for growth and development. Use them as a valuable tool for improving your skills and confidence. Try to view each failure as a step toward your goals. Learning from mistakes helps you become more adaptable and resilient to change, which ultimately leads you to greater success. Don't fear mistakes; instead, see them as an integral part of your journey toward success, and you will find that each failure brings you closer to your dreams.

Creating a Competitive Advantage

Paying attention to details can become your competitive advantage. What may seem insignificant to others could be the key to your success.

Example: Elon Musk, an entrepreneur and inventor, is known for his attention to detail in projects such as SpaceX and Tesla. His approach to meticulously refining details and continuous improvement has allowed him to achieve outstanding results in highly competitive industries.

To achieve sustainable success in any area of business or life, it is important not only to follow best practices but also to find ways to create a unique advantage over competitors. In this chapter, we will explore strategies and methods that can help you stand out from the competition and achieve success.

Competitor Analysis

1. Identifying Competitors: To create an advantage, you first need to understand who your competitors are. These can be direct competitors offering similar products or services, as well as indirect ones that address the same problem in different ways.

Example: If you are launching a new fitness app, your competitors may include other fitness apps, as well as gyms and online fitness courses.

2. Analyzing Strengths and Weaknesses: Study what your competitors do well and where they have shortcomings. This will help you identify opportunities for improvement and niche segments to explore.

Example: Netflix researched what makes traditional television channels successful and noticed that many of them had limited programming. This insight allowed them to create a platform with unlimited content options and offer users greater flexibility.

Unique Selling Proposition (USP)

1. Defining the USP: Create a unique selling proposition that differentiates your product or service from the competition. The USP should be clear and concise so that potential customers can easily understand why they should choose you.

Example: Apple stands out in the mobile phone market due to its unique design, innovative features, and ecosystem integration. Their USP is that users can enjoy a seamless experience across various company products.

2. Communicating the USP: Effectively communicate your USP through marketing channels. This can include advertising, social media, content marketing, and other promotional forms.

Example: Starbucks Starbucks distinguishes itself in the coffee shop market through a unique customer service culture and a high degree of personalization. They actively promote this unique selling proposition (USP) in their advertising materials and on social media.

Innovation and Continuous Improvement

1. Implementing Innovations: Innovations can be a powerful tool for creating a competitive advantage. This may include adopting new technologies, improving products and services, or developing unique business models.

Example: Tesla continually implements innovations in its electric vehicles, including autonomous driving and improved batteries. These innovations help them stand out from traditional automobile manufacturers.

2. Continuous Improvement: Regularly updating and enhancing your offerings helps maintain competitiveness. Customer feedback and market analysis can help you identify areas for improvement.

Example: Amazon continuously improves its platform by adding new features, enhancing the user interface, and expanding its product range. This enables them to maintain leadership in e-commerce.

Quality and Customer Service

1. Ensuring High Quality: High-quality products and services are foundational for creating a competitive advantage. Customers are willing to pay more for reliable and quality solutions.

Example: Rolex has succeeded in the watch market due to impeccable quality and prestige. Their watches are known for their reliability and durability, allowing them to command high prices and stand out from competitors.

2. Excellent Customer Service: Customer service can be a key factor that distinguishes you from competitors. Outstanding service helps build loyalty and increase customer satisfaction.

Example: Zappos, a shoe and clothing retailer, is known for its exceptional customer service. They offer free returns and 24/7 support, significantly enhancing the customer experience and fostering loyalty.

Strategic Partnerships

1. Creating Partnerships: Partnering with other companies or organizations can help strengthen your competitive advantage. This may include joint projects, marketing campaigns, or resource sharing.

Example: Starbucks and Spotify partnered to create a unique music experience in Starbucks cafes, attracting new customers and strengthening the brand of both companies.

2. Establishing Long-Term Relationships: Working with partners on a long-term basis can lead to sustainable competitive advantages. Long-term relationships help create joint strategies and enhance mutual interests.

Example: Google and smartphone manufacturers like Samsung have long-term partnerships that contribute to the development of new technologies and enhance the user experience on Android devices.

Creating a competitive advantage requires careful analysis, innovation, high quality, and a strategic approach. These elements work together to help you stand out from competitors and achieve success in your chosen field. Let's start with analysis. A deep understanding of the market, its needs, and trends is fundamental for making informed decisions. This includes researching your target audience, identifying their preferences, and studying competitor actions. This approach allows you to identify opportunities and threats that may affect your business.

Innovation plays a key role in creating competitive advantages. It can take various forms: from new products and services to improving existing processes and methods of operation. It's important not only to generate ideas but also to implement them successfully. This requires openness to new technologies and a willingness to experiment and learn from mistakes. Innovations not only make your product or service unique but also help you respond to market changes.

Quality is another important aspect. In a highly competitive environment, consumers are increasingly demanding about what they purchase. Ensuring high-quality products and services helps earn customer trust and build long-term relationships. It also serves as a foundation for a positive reputation, which can be a powerful tool for attracting new customers. Maintaining high standards requires a systematic approach and constant quality control at all levels of the business.

A strategic approach integrates all these elements. Developing a clear strategy allows you to set priorities and allocate resources to maximize efficiency. It also involves planning actions based on data analysis and forecasts, helping you adapt to changing market conditions. Without a strategy, your efforts may be disjointed and insufficiently focused.

It's important to remember that successfully creating and maintaining a competitive advantage requires continuous market analysis and adaptation to changes. The market is dynamic, and new trends or technologies can quickly alter the landscape. Regular monitoring of the situation allows you to respond to changes in a timely manner, adjust your actions, and maintain the relevance of your offerings. Such a proactive approach not only contributes to survival but also to the prosperity of your business in an environment of constant uncertainty.

Thus, creating a competitive advantage is a complex process that requires integrating analysis, innovation, quality, and a strategic approach. By paying attention to each of these aspects, you can not only stand out from competitors but also achieve sustainable success in your field. Remember, in the business world, initiative is important, but so is the ability to adapt to new conditions and challenges, which will ultimately be the key to your success.

Practical Steps for Applying the Magic of Details

1. Set Clear Goals: Identify which details are most important for achieving your goals. Break down your larger goals into smaller, manageable tasks and focus on completing them.

2. Develop a Tracking System: Create a system for tracking your small steps and details. This can be a journal, an app, or simply a task list. Regularly review your achievements and adjust your actions as needed.

3. Continuous Improvement: Strive for continuous improvement in the details. Evaluate what you can enhance in your daily activities and implement changes to boost your efficiency.

4. Feedback: Seek feedback on your actions and pay attention to details that can be improved. Use this information to adjust your actions and strategy.

The magic of details lies in the fact that even the smallest details and steps can significantly impact your path to success. In today's world, where competition is growing and demands are becoming increasingly high, attention to detail takes on special significance. This can be something simple, like thoroughly planning your tasks or improving specific aspects of your project. Such actions may seem insignificant, but ultimately, they can lead to substantial results. Attention to detail helps avoid mistakes, achieve big goals, and create competitive advantages that set you apart from others.

It is important to recognize that success often consists of many small steps that you take each day. Every element of your process, every detail, can influence the overall outcome. For example, careful attention to detail in your work helps avoid common mistakes and significantly enhances the quality of the final product. When you pay attention to the little things, you create a foundation for achieving big results.

Moreover, attention to detail helps you develop confidence in your abilities. When you take the time to work through the details, you become more assured in your actions and decisions. This contributes to increased efficiency and allows you to handle emerging challenges more effectively. The small achievements you document along your path strengthen your belief in your own capabilities and motivate you to move forward.

It's also worth remembering that the little things can be a source of inspiration. When you begin to notice and appreciate the details, you open yourself up to new opportunities and ideas. This can lead to improved processes or the emergence of new strategies that help you achieve success. Your ability to notice and analyze the minutiae allows you to stay one step ahead and adapt to changing circumstances.

Additionally, it's crucial to understand that attention to detail creates a positive impression on others. When you demonstrate thoroughness and care for every aspect of your work, it fosters trust and respect from colleagues and clients. People value quality and professionalism, and your commitment to the small details can become your competitive advantage.

Pay attention to the little things, and you will see how they can transform your dreams into reality. Every small step and every detail matters and can serve as the foundation for significant changes. Remember that success is not only about major achievements but also about the ability to notice and utilize every little thing along your journey. Ultimately, it is the attention to detail that creates a solid foundation for your success and enables you to move forward with confidence and determination.

Chapter 16:
Tools for Success

In today's world, there is a vast array of tools and technologies that can significantly ease your path to success. This chapter is dedicated to how to choose and use the most effective tools to enhance productivity, organize your work, and achieve your goals.

Time Management Technologies

Calendar Programs
Calendar programs, such as Google Calendar or Microsoft Outlook, allow you to organize your time and plan tasks. You can create events, set reminders, and share your plans with others.

Example: Google Calendar enables integration with other applications and sends reminders to your mobile device, making it easier to manage your time and meet deadlines.

Time Trackers
Time tracking software, such as Toggl or Clockify, helps you monitor how much time you spend on various tasks. This allows you to identify areas where you can optimize your efforts.

Example: Toggl lets you create projects and tasks, track time, and analyze reports to see where your time goes and how you can become more efficient.

Productivity Tools

Task Lists and Task Managers
Applications for creating task lists, such as Todoist or Microsoft To Do, help organize and prioritize your tasks. They allow you to create subtasks, set deadlines, and send reminders.

Example: Todoist offers features for creating projects, setting deadlines and reminders, as well as sharing tasks with other users and tracking completion.

Focusing Apps
Programs like Focus@Will or Pomodoro Timer help you concentrate on your work by using time management techniques, such as the Pomodoro

Technique. This can enhance your focus and productivity.

Example: Pomodoro Timer assists in breaking your work time into intervals, promoting sustained productivity and preventing burnout.

Planning and Strategy Tools

Idea Visualization Platforms
Mind mapping and idea visualization tools, such as MindMeister or XMind, help structure your thoughts and ideas. This is useful for project planning and strategy development.

Example: MindMeister allows you to create visual maps of ideas, helping organize thoughts, plan projects, and work on strategies in a more convenient and understandable form.

Project Management Platforms
Project management systems, such as Asana or Trello, help organize tasks, track their completion, and collaborate with the team. These tools offer features for creating task boards, setting deadlines, and managing resources.

Example: Trello uses visual boards and cards for project management, making it easier to track progress and collaborate on tasks.

Personal Development Tools

Education and Training Apps
Online learning platforms, such as Coursera or Udemy, offer courses and training on various topics to help you develop skills and enhance your qualifications.

Example: Coursera provides access to courses from leading universities and organizations, allowing you to learn at your convenience and develop the necessary skills to achieve your goals.

Meditation and Relaxation Apps
Tools like Headspace or Calm help manage stress and maintain mental health. These apps offer meditations, breathing exercises, and relaxation practices.

Example: Headspace provides a variety of meditations and practices to increase mindfulness and manage stress, which contributes to improved focus and productivity.

Communication and Collaboration Tools

Video Conferencing Systems

Video conferencing tools, such as Zoom or Microsoft Teams, enable you to hold meetings and negotiations remotely. This is convenient for communicating with clients, partners, and team members.

Example: Zoom allows for video calls, webinars, and online meetings with participants around the world, simplifying communication and collaboration.

Collaboration Platforms
Collaboration tools, such as Slack or Google Workspace, help teams effectively share information and work on projects in real-time.

Example: Slack offers channels for communication, integration with other tools, and file-sharing capabilities, which facilitate collaboration and communication within a team.

Proper use of tools and technologies can significantly enhance your productivity, organization, and efficiency. In today's world, where the flow of information and tasks is constantly increasing, it's crucial to find ways to optimize your work. Choosing tools that best align with your goals and needs becomes a key aspect of successfully completing tasks. This may include project management software, time management applications, or collaboration tools.

Integrating selected tools into your daily activities helps create a systematic approach to work organization. When technology becomes a part of your workflow, it simplifies task execution, allows for better progress tracking, and significantly reduces time spent on routine activities. This frees up resources for more important and creative tasks, which, in turn, contributes to overall productivity.

It is also important to regularly assess the effectiveness of the tools you use. The technology landscape is rapidly changing, and what was relevant yesterday may become ineffective today. Pay attention to which tools provide real benefits and which ones turn out to be less useful. This evaluation will allow you to adapt in a timely manner and find new solutions that can enhance your work.

Additionally, proper use of technology requires training and adaptation. You need to dedicate time to learn about all the features of the tools to fully unlock their potential. Investing effort into training will not only help you handle tasks more quickly but also enable you to apply new functions that can significantly improve your work.

Chapter 17:
Secrets of Personal Effectiveness

Effectiveness is not just the ability to perform tasks, but also the skill of using your time and energy optimally to achieve maximum results. In this chapter, we will explore the key aspects of personal effectiveness, ways to manage energy, and strategies to boost productivity.

Definition of Personal Effectiveness

What is Personal Effectiveness?
Personal effectiveness encompasses the ability to achieve desired outcomes while optimally utilizing resources such as time, energy, and skills. It involves the capacity to prioritize, organize work, and focus on tasks that deliver the greatest value.

Example: An effective person can handle multiple tasks simultaneously without losing focus or quality of work.

Personal effectiveness is the ability to achieve set goals and objectives while optimizing the use of time, resources, and efforts. It is a key characteristic of successful people, enabling them to achieve high results, maintain a balance between work and personal life, and minimize stress and burnout. In this section, we will examine in detail what personal effectiveness includes, how it can be measured, and how it can be developed.

Components of Personal Effectiveness

Time Management
Effective people are skilled at allocating their time rationally by identifying priority tasks and avoiding procrastination. They utilize various techniques and tools for planning and organizing their workflow.

Example: Setting clear deadlines for task completion, using planners and calendars, helps manage time effectively.

Energy Management
Energy is a resource that can be distributed across various tasks. Personal energy management involves understanding one's own biological rhythms, scheduling tasks based on energy levels, and applying strategies to maintain high productivity.

Example: Tackling the most challenging tasks in the morning when energy levels are highest and saving lighter tasks for the afternoon when energy may decline.

Workspace Organization
Creating a comfortable and organized workspace helps minimize distractions and enhances concentration on task completion. Effective individuals pay attention to their workspace to foster productive work habits.

Example: An open, well-lit space with a neatly organized desk and minimal clutter can significantly boost productivity.

Skill and Knowledge Development
Continuous development and updating of skills and knowledge help maintain competitiveness and effectively tackle new challenges. Personal effectiveness is closely related to learning and self-improvement.

Example: Participating in professional development courses and reading books on career advancement enhance skills and boost competence.

Goal Setting and Planning
Clear goal setting and creating action plans are fundamental to personal effectiveness. Effective individuals set specific, measurable, and achievable goals and develop strategies to reach them.

Example: Using the SMART method for goal setting helps create clear and realistic plans that can be effectively executed.

Measuring Personal Effectiveness

Qualitative and Quantitative Indicators
Measuring personal effectiveness can include both quantitative and qualitative indicators. Quantitative indicators may include the number of tasks completed, deadlines met, and results achieved. Qualitative indicators may include satisfaction with completed work and the degree of control over stress.

Example: Tracking the number of projects completed on time and assessing satisfaction with the work done helps determine effectiveness levels.

Regular Self-Assessment
Self-assessment and self-evaluation help identify strengths and weaknesses, as well as understand how to improve personal effectiveness.

Regular reflection on successes and failures aids in adjusting strategies and approaches.

Example: Keeping a self-assessment journal that records achievements and areas for improvement allows for an objective evaluation of one's results.

Developing Personal Effectiveness

Setting Specific Goals
Developing and implementing specific goals, both in the short and long term, helps focus on significant tasks and achieve desired results. Clear goals serve as motivation and guidance throughout the work process.
Example: Setting a goal to increase sales by 20% in the upcoming quarter and creating an action plan to achieve this goal.

Using Tools and Techniques
Using Various Tools and Techniques for Time, Task, and Project Management

The use of various tools and techniques for managing time, tasks, and projects helps enhance effectiveness. Technological solutions, such as planning and task automation applications, play a significant role in optimizing workflows.

Example: Utilizing a project management application like Asana or Trello to track progress and coordinate tasks.

Continuous Learning and Adaptation
Personal effectiveness requires continuous learning and adaptation to changing conditions. Openness to new methods and approaches, along with a willingness to learn and adapt, helps maintain a high level of productivity and achieve new heights.

Example: Participating in training on personal effectiveness and implementing new approaches to improve workflow.

Personal effectiveness is a key aspect of a successful life and career, encompassing numerous elements such as time and energy management, workspace organization, skill development, and goal setting. Each of these components plays a crucial role in shaping productivity and achieving set objectives. Recognizing the importance of these aspects allows for not only optimizing one's actions but also creating conditions for sustainable growth and success.

Time Management is the foundation of personal effectiveness. The ability to prioritize and allocate time among tasks helps avoid stress and achieve more. It is important not only to monitor schedules but also to understand which tasks truly matter for reaching your goals. Defining time limits and monitoring task completion contribute to more rational resource use.

Energy is another crucial factor affecting your productivity. Understanding your biological rhythms and peak activity times allows you to find the optimal times for tackling the most challenging tasks. Regular breaks and rejuvenation help maintain a high energy level throughout the day, significantly enhancing your ability to focus and work effectively.

Workspace Organization also plays an important role in increasing personal effectiveness. A clean and organized environment promotes concentration and reduces distractions. It is essential to create a space where you feel comfortable and can work efficiently. Proper organization of tools and materials minimizes the time spent searching for what you need and allows you to focus on completing tasks.

Skill Development is a continuous process that requires attention and effort. Ongoing learning and self-improvement open new horizons and opportunities. The ability to adapt to new conditions and technologies helps maintain competitiveness and confidently move forward in your career. Self-development not only enhances qualifications but also fosters personal growth, making you more self-assured in your abilities.

Goal Setting is an important aspect that determines the direction of your movement. Clearly defined goals help you focus on what matters and avoid unnecessary distractions. Developing a plan to achieve these goals and regularly monitoring progress allows you to maintain motivation and confidence throughout your journey.

By employing the methods and strategies described, you can significantly improve your personal effectiveness. Awareness and development of these components will help you become more productive, achieve your goals, and enhance your quality of life. Personal effectiveness is not just a set of skills but a comprehensive approach that requires attention and ongoing practice. Ultimately, working on yourself and improving personal effectiveness will open new horizons and opportunities, leading to success in any endeavor.

How is Personal Effectiveness Measured?
Measuring personal effectiveness can be subjective and objective.

Objective indicators include completing tasks on time, achieving goals, and fulfilling plans. Subjective criteria may include the feeling of satisfaction from completed work and the level of stress.

Example: If you successfully complete all tasks on your daily list and feel satisfied, this may be a sign of high personal effectiveness.

Time Management

Pomodoro Technique

The Pomodoro Technique involves working for 25 minutes, followed by a 5-minute break. After four such cycles, a longer break is taken. This method helps maintain focus and prevents burnout.

Example: Using a timer to set work and rest intervals can significantly increase productivity and reduce fatigue.

Planning and Prioritization

Creating a task list and prioritizing will help you focus on the most important and urgent matters. Using techniques such as the Eisenhower Matrix helps categorize tasks by importance and urgency.

Example: First, tackle tasks that are both highly important and urgent, and then move on to less significant tasks.

Energy Management

Developing Good Habits

Physical health directly influences your personal effectiveness. Regular exercise, a balanced diet, and sufficient sleep help maintain high levels of energy and concentration.

Example: Morning workouts and balanced nutrition can enhance your productivity throughout the day.

Stress Management

Learn to manage stress using relaxation techniques such as meditation or deep breathing. This will help you stay calm in tense situations and avoid burnout.

Example: Daily meditation practice helps reduce stress levels and improves focus.

Stress Management: Key Strategies and Practices

Stress management is a vital aspect of personal effectiveness and overall well-being. Stress, in moderation, can be a motivating factor, but excessive or chronic stress can negatively impact health, productivity, and quality of life. In this section, we will delve into stress management strategies and practices that will help you maintain harmony and productivity.

Understanding Stress
Nature of Stress
Stress is the body's reaction to external or internal stimuli perceived as threats or challenges. In response to a stressor, the body activates the "fight" or "flight" response, which may manifest as physical, emotional, and psychological strain.

Example: External stressors may include work deadlines or family issues, while internal stressors may be related to self-criticism or high expectations from oneself.

Types of Stress

Acute Stress and Chronic Stress
Acute Stress: Short-term stress that arises in response to specific events, such as public speaking or handling urgent tasks.
Chronic Stress: Long-term stress that can develop from ongoing issues, such as job failures or persistent family conflicts.

Stress Management Strategies
Physical Activity
Regular physical exercise promotes the production of endorphins, which help reduce stress levels and improve overall well-being. Physical activity also enhances sleep quality and increases energy levels.

Example: Walking outdoors, participating in sports, practicing yoga, or even short workouts can effectively lower stress levels.

Relaxation Techniques
Relaxation techniques help reduce physical and emotional tension. These can include deep breathing methods, meditation, progressive muscle relaxation, and other practices aimed at relaxation.

Example: Practicing meditation for 10-15 minutes each day can calm the mind and reduce anxiety levels.

Time Organization

Effective time management and task planning help reduce stress associated with deadlines and overloads.
Proper time allocation and prioritization help prevent task accumulation and feelings of being overwhelmed.

Example: Using the Pomodoro Technique, where work is divided into 25-minute intervals with short breaks, can help maintain focus and avoid stress from long work sessions.

Social Support
Communicating with family, friends, and colleagues can provide support and alleviate stress. Conversations with those who understand your concerns can help you feel less lonely and more confident.

Example: Regular gatherings with friends or participating in group activities help create a supportive environment and reduce stress levels.

Healthy Lifestyle
A healthy diet, adequate sleep, and the avoidance of harmful habits contribute to overall well-being and increased resilience to stress. A healthy lifestyle strengthens the body and improves the ability to cope with challenges.

Example: Maintaining a sleep schedule, eating a balanced diet, and avoiding alcohol and smoking can help sustain high energy levels and reduce stress.

Psychological Approaches to Stress Management
Cognitive Behavioral Therapy (CBT)
CBT helps change negative thought patterns and behaviors that contribute to stress. The therapy focuses on identifying and modifying dysfunctional thoughts and behaviors.

Example: Working with a therapist to reframe negative thoughts and develop a more positive outlook on situations.

Acceptance and Mindfulness
Acceptance and mindfulness help individuals perceive stressful situations as a part of life and respond to them more calmly. Mindfulness involves paying attention to the present moment and accepting one's emotions and thoughts without judgment.

Example: Practicing mindfulness, such as being aware of your breathing and sensations, can reduce reactivity to stressful events.

Setting Realistic Goals
Establishing achievable and realistic goals helps prevent feelings of being overwhelmed and stressed. A clear understanding of one's capabilities and limitations aids in more effective planning and task management.

Example: Setting goals that align with your available resources and time helps avoid unrealistic expectations and reduces stress.

Stress Management as a Comprehensive Process
Stress management is a complex process that includes various elements contributing to improved physical and mental well-being. Physical activity plays a vital role in lowering stress levels. Regular exercise helps release endorphins, which improve mood and decrease feelings of anxiety. Physical activity also enables the body to handle accumulated tension, leading to overall well-being.

Relaxation techniques, such as deep breathing, meditation, or yoga, are effective ways to cope with stress. These methods help calm the mind and relax the body, reducing tension and enhancing emotional state. Regular use of relaxation techniques can become an essential tool in stress management and increasing resilience.

Time organization is another key aspect of stress management. Effective task planning prevents overloads and facilitates more rational resource use. The ability to prioritize and break larger tasks into smaller steps helps reduce anxiety and ensures confidence in completing goals. This creates a sense of control and improves overall well-being.

Social support also plays a crucial role in stress management. Interacting with friends, family, or colleagues can help alleviate anxiety and provide emotional support. Sharing your thoughts and feelings with loved ones can lead to not only support but also new perspectives on your problems. Social connections foster a safe space for openly discussing your experiences.

A healthy lifestyle is a fundamental element of stress management. A balanced diet, sufficient sleep, and the avoidance of harmful habits contribute to maintaining physical and mental health. Caring for your body allows you to better handle stressors and maintain energy levels, which are essential factors in stress management.

Psychological approaches, such as cognitive behavioral therapy and mindfulness, help address internal sources of stress. These methods aim to change negative thought patterns and develop skills for recognizing one's emotions and reactions. Mindfulness enables you to stay present and prevents stress from overwhelming your mind, while cognitive behavioral therapy helps you develop more adaptive responses to stressful situations.

Applying all these strategies in combination will not only help you reduce stress levels but also enhance overall productivity and quality of life. Stress management is a process that requires continuous attention and practice, but the efforts invested will yield significant dividends in terms of improved emotional well-being and greater self-confidence.

Skill Development and Learning
Continuous Learning
Ongoing development of professional and personal skills contributes to increased effectiveness. Reading books, taking courses, and participating in training sessions can help you expand your knowledge and improve your skills.

Continuous Learning
Example: Courses on project management or public speaking can enhance your competence and boost your confidence.

Feedback and Self-Analysis
Regular self-analysis and feedback from colleagues or mentors can help you identify your weaknesses and work on improving them.

Example: Regular meetings with a mentor or colleagues to discuss completed projects can provide valuable insights and recommendations for improvement.

Creating an Effective Workspace

Organizing Your Workspace
Create a workspace that fosters concentration and productivity. Ensure that your workspace is comfortable, organized, and free from distractions.

Example: A comfortable chair, a clean desk, and minimizing noise in your workspace can significantly improve your productivity.

Planning Your Workspace

Defining Workspace Goals
Before organizing your workspace, it's important to define the tasks you will perform and the requirements for your workspace. This will help you create a space that meets your needs.

Example: If your job requires frequent computer use, you will need a comfortable desk and chair, as well as enough space for additional equipment.

Zoning the Workspace

Dividing your workspace into different zones (e.g., work zone, storage zone, and relaxation zone) helps organize the space more effectively and maintain order.

Example: Allocate a separate zone for documents and stationery, as well as for storing personal items, to avoid clutter on your desk.

Choosing Furniture and Equipment

Comfortable Office Furniture
Choosing quality and comfortable office furniture is a key element in organizing your workspace. A comfortable chair and ergonomic desk can help you maintain proper posture and reduce physical strain.

Example: Investing in an adjustable chair that supports your back can help prevent spine issues and reduce fatigue.

Equipment and Technology
Proper placement of equipment, such as computers, printers, and phones, as well as ensuring access to necessary technology, contributes to increased productivity.

Example: Make sure all cables and wires are neatly arranged and do not obstruct your work process by using cable organizers.

Organizing Storage

Convenient Document Storage
Organizing storage systems for documents and stationery helps maintain order and avoid losing important materials. Use filing cabinets, folders, and organizers.

Example: Categorizing documents and labeling folders can help you quickly find the materials you need and keep everything organized.

Minimalism and Order
Reducing the number of unnecessary items on your desk and regularly clearing your workspace of unneeded things contribute to creating a more productive environment.

Example: Regularly review the contents of drawers and shelves, getting rid of outdated or unnecessary materials.

Adapting to Your Needs

Personalizing Your Workspace
Adding elements that create a comfortable atmosphere, such as plants, photos, or items you like, helps make your workspace more enjoyable.

Example: Placing small green plants on your desk can not only enhance the atmosphere but also positively impact your mood and productivity.

Adapting to Work Processes
Consider that your work process may change over time, and your workspace should adapt to these changes. Regularly update and improve your workspace according to your evolving needs.

Example: If you start working on new projects, you may need more space for materials or new equipment.

Creating a Comfortable Atmosphere Lighting

Proper lighting plays a crucial role in creating a comfortable work environment. Use both natural and artificial lighting to ensure optimal brightness levels.

Example: Position your desk near a window to maximize natural light and use a desk lamp with adjustable brightness for evening work.

Temperature and Ventilation
Comfortable temperature and good ventilation help maintain productivity and prevent fatigue. Regularly air out your workspace and monitor the temperature.

Example: Use fans or heaters to maintain optimal temperature depending on the season and your preferences.

Conclusion
Organizing your workspace is not just about creating a functional area; it's about forming conditions that contribute to your comfort and productivity. The importance of comfortable furniture cannot be underestimated; it impacts your well-being and energy levels throughout the workday. Choosing a chair and desk that suit your physique and work habits helps avoid physical discomfort and enhances your ability to focus on tasks.

Effective storage is another key aspect of workspace organization. Well-ordered documents, tools, and materials not only create visual order but also allow you to quickly locate necessary items. This reduces stress associated with searching for and organizing materials and helps you maintain productivity.

Maintaining Focus on Current Tasks
Smart use of drawers, shelves, and organizers contributes to creating a more structured work environment. Personalizing your workspace is significant for creating an atmosphere that inspires and motivates. Elements such as photos, plants, or items reflecting your interests can make your workspace cozier and more appealing. This not only helps you feel more comfortable but also contributes to a positive emotional backdrop, which, in turn, enhances productivity.

Attention to details such as lighting and ventilation also plays a key role in organizing your workspace. Good lighting helps reduce eye fatigue and improves mood. Natural light, if possible, is the ideal option, but using quality artificial light sources can be a good alternative. Ventilation is important for maintaining fresh air and comfort, which affects energy levels and overall productivity.

Creating the perfect workspace requires a comprehensive approach that considers all the aforementioned factors. Applying these principles will help you boost productivity, improve mood, and create conditions for successful work. Ultimately, an organized and comfortable workspace becomes not only a foundation for achieving professional goals but also an essential element of overall well-being.

Using Technology for Automation
Utilizing technology and tools for automating routine tasks can free up time for more meaningful projects. Workflow automation and task management programs can help optimize your processes.

Example: Automating reports and reminders with specialized software can save time and reduce errors.

Personal Development and Motivation Goal Setting and Self-Motivation

Setting clear goals and creating an action plan helps maintain motivation and focus on results. Regularly reviewing your goals and achievements contributes to sustained motivation.

Example: Keeping a success journal of small victories can help maintain your motivation and remind you of your progress.

Rewarding Yourself
Regularly rewarding yourself for achieving goals helps maintain a positive attitude toward work and increases satisfaction with the process.

Example: Allow yourself small pleasures after completing important tasks to keep your motivation high and enjoy the work.

Self-Reward: How to Motivate and Reward Yourself for Achieving Goals
Self-rewarding is an important aspect of self-management and goal achievement. Regularly rewarding yourself for achievements helps maintain motivation, strengthens self-confidence, and makes the work process more enjoyable. In this chapter, we will explore how to reward yourself effectively to achieve your goals and maintain high levels of motivation.

Understanding the Importance of Rewarding

Why Rewarding Is Important
Rewarding plays a key role in sustaining motivation and reinforcing positive habits. It helps solidify successful behavior and creates a positive association with achieving goals.

Example: If you successfully complete a project, rewarding yourself with a dinner out or buying something you've wanted can help maintain your drive for success in the future.

How Rewarding Influences Motivation
Proper rewarding not only strengthens your commitment to goals but also makes the process more enjoyable. It allows you to celebrate your achievements and motivates you to keep moving forward.

Example: Set small goals and reward yourself for each achievement. This will help maintain high levels of motivation and make the goal achievement process more engaging.

Types of Rewards

Intrinsic Rewards
Intrinsic rewards include feelings of satisfaction, pride, and joy from completing work. They can become powerful motivators if you learn to recognize and appreciate them.

Example: After completing a challenging task or achieving an important goal, take time for self-reflection and acknowledge your efforts. Write down how you feel and what it means to you.

Extrinsic Rewards
Extrinsic rewards can include material rewards or activities that bring pleasure. These can be gifts, days off, or special events.

Example: If you achieve a significant goal, reward yourself by buying something you've wanted for a long time or spending a day at a nice place.

Choosing Appropriate Rewards

Matching Rewards to Goals
An important aspect is selecting rewards that align with your goals and motivation. Rewards should be appealing enough to motivate you to take action.

Example: If your goal is related to improving health, reward yourself with a visit to a spa or activities you enjoy.

Proportionality of Rewards and Achievements
Rewards should be proportional to the level of achievement. This helps maintain balance and prevents loss of motivation in the long term.

Example: For small achievements, choose small rewards, like time for your favorite hobby, while for larger goals, opt for more significant rewards, such as a trip or a major purchase.

Creating a Reward System

Setting Motivational Goals
Create a system where you set clear goals and match them with specific rewards. This will help you maintain motivation and track progress.

Example: Create a chart or diagram where you track achieved goals and planned rewards. This will help you visualize progress and sustain motivation.

Regular Check-Ins and Adjustments

Regularly Reviewing and Adjusting Your Reward System
Regularly review and adjust your reward system to keep it relevant and effective. Ensure that your rewards continue to motivate you and align with your achievements.

Example: Every few months, reassess your goals and rewards to ensure they remain motivating and meet your current needs and desires.

Examples of Effective

Rewarding Success Stories
Look at examples of successful individuals who have used rewards to achieve their goals. Learn how they motivated themselves and what methods they employed.

Example: Brenй Brown, a renowned researcher and author, uses the method of rewards in her practice and teaching, emphasizing the importance of recognizing one's achievements.

Personal Stories
Share your own stories and examples of how you used rewards to achieve your goals. This will help you understand what works for you and which methods are most effective.

Example: After achieving a significant business goal, I rewarded myself with a weekend trip to a place I had always wanted to visit. This not only boosted my motivation but also helped me recharge.

The Importance of Self-Rewarding
Rewarding yourself is a crucial aspect of maintaining motivation and achieving goals. This process helps create positive reinforcement that drives you forward and enables you to overcome challenges. Choosing the right intrinsic and extrinsic rewards requires attention and awareness of your preferences. Intrinsic rewards can include feelings of satisfaction from completing a task or joy from progress, while extrinsic rewards may be related to physical rewards, such as relaxation or small gifts.

Creating a system for implementing rewards helps make the process more structured and predictable. This can be a simple framework where you define specific achievements and their corresponding rewards. For example, you might reward yourself for completing a project by dedicating time to a favorite hobby or purchasing something you desire. This approach not only allows you to acknowledge your achievements but also creates additional motivation for achieving them.

Regularly reviewing your reward methods is also essential. What worked previously may lose its appeal over time, so it's important to stay open to new ideas and approaches. By analyzing which rewards bring the most satisfaction and motivation, you can adapt your system to ensure it remains effective and relevant.

Using rewards helps you stay motivated and engaged in the goal achievement process. Applying this approach makes the journey to success more enjoyable, turning challenging moments into opportunities for self-reward and celebration of progress. Ultimately, regular rewards contribute to creating a positive atmosphere where you can not only achieve your goals but also enjoy the process itself.

Personal Effectiveness
Personal effectiveness is a comprehensive process that encompasses various aspects of your life and work. Time management is one of the key elements that allows you to organize your tasks and resources to maximize results. Effective time allocation helps avoid overloads and promotes a more rational use of each day.

Energy also plays an important role in personal effectiveness. Being aware of your energy peaks and managing your physical and mental energy allows you to work more productively. Maintaining a high level of energy includes regular breaks, physical activity, and caring for your health, which in turn contributes to better focus and productivity.

Skill development is another important aspect that helps you adapt to changing conditions and enhance your competitiveness. Continuous learning and self-development open new horizons and opportunities for growth. The ability to accumulate and apply new knowledge makes you more confident and effective in completing tasks.

Creating a productive workspace also significantly impacts your personal effectiveness. A comfortable organization of the space, including proper lighting and material storage, promotes improved concentration and reduces stress levels. A comfortable and structured environment helps you focus on tasks and achieve your goals.

By applying the strategies and techniques outlined in this chapter, you can significantly enhance your productivity. Each of these elements plays a vital role in shaping your overall level of effectiveness and success. Striving for continuous improvement in all these aspects will help you achieve better results and become more successful in your endeavors, regardless of the field of activity.

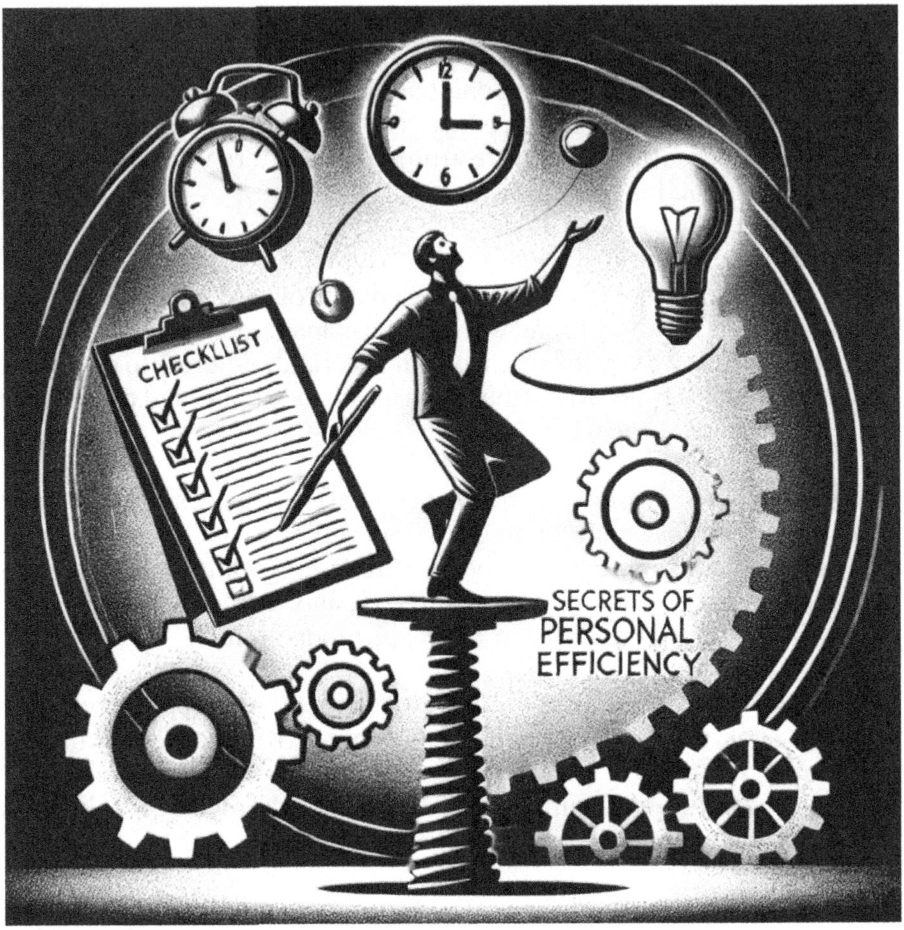
CHECKLLIST
SECRETS OF
PERSONAL
EFFICIENCY

Chapter 18:
The Power of Acknowledgment

How to Celebrate Your Successes and Use Them as Motivation for New Achievements

Celebrating your successes and victories is not only enjoyable but also essential for maintaining motivation and achieving new goals. This chapter is dedicated to how to properly celebrate your achievements and how to use them as a powerful source of inspiration for future accomplishments. We will explore why it's important to celebrate your successes, how to do it effectively, and which methods will help you derive maximum benefit from your achievements.

The Importance of Celebrating Successes

Why It Matters
Celebrating successes helps reinforce feelings of satisfaction and pride in your accomplishments. It also boosts self-esteem and strengthens self-confidence, which is necessary for overcoming future challenges.

Example: If you complete a significant project at work, celebrating that achievement can become a source of joy and motivation. It allows you to enjoy the result and feel your worth.

How Celebration Affects Motivation
When you celebrate your achievements, you create positive associations with the work process and goal attainment. This helps maintain high motivation and a positive attitude toward future tasks.

Example: When athletes win competitions, they not only receive medals but also host celebrations that help reinforce their motivation and readiness for new achievements.

How Celebration Influences Motivation
Celebrating successes is not just a pleasant ritual but an important aspect of motivation management. When we acknowledge and celebrate our achievements, it profoundly impacts our internal state and readiness for new challenges. In this section, we will explore how celebrating successes contributes to motivation and how to leverage this process to maintain high performance.

Creating Positive Associations
Psychological Effect

Celebrating successes creates positive associations with the process of achieving goals. Every time you celebrate a victory, you reinforce a positive attitude toward what you do. This helps form a connection in your mind between effort and reward.

Example: If you successfully complete a major project and celebrate that achievement, your brain retains the positive emotions associated with that success. The next time you encounter difficulties, your subconscious will strive to repeat those positive feelings.

Emotional Reinforcement
Celebrating achievements enhances positive emotions and satisfaction from the work done. These emotions can become a strong motivator for continuing work and achieving new goals.

Example: When an athlete wins a competition and receives a medal, it brings not only pride but also joy, which strengthens their desire to continue training and achieve new victories.

Strengthening Self-Esteem and Confidence
Boosting Self-Esteem
Celebrating successes reinforces your self-esteem and confidence in your abilities. When you acknowledge and celebrate your achievements, you show yourself and others that you are capable of achieving set goals.

Example: When an entrepreneur sees the successful development of their business and celebrates it, they reinforce their belief in their capabilities, which helps them tackle new challenges and make bolder decisions.

Motivation through Achievements
Successes become a source of additional motivation. Seeing that your efforts lead to results makes you more interested and motivated to achieve the next goals.

Example: After a successful product launch, a team in a company celebrates their success, creating an atmosphere of enthusiasm and eagerness for the next project.

Creating a Cycle of Motivation
Positive Cycle
Celebrating successes initiates a positive cycle: successfully completing one project leads to motivation for starting the next. Each success becomes a stepping stone toward achieving new goals.

Example: When a writer completes a book and holds a launch event, that success motivates them to start working on a new piece, maintaining a high level of productivity.

Systematic Approach
Creating a systematic approach to celebrating successes helps maintain motivation over the long term. Regular celebrations and acknowledgements of achieved goals create a sustainable cycle of motivation and satisfaction.

Example: In a large company, employees regularly celebrate quarterly successes and achievements, maintaining a high level of motivation and team spirit throughout the year.

Skills and Opportunities for Development
Uncovering New Opportunities
Celebrating successes can reveal new opportunities and ideas for further development. Acknowledging and celebrating achievements can serve as a source of inspiration for seeking new paths and possibilities.

Example: After successfully completing one project, the team analyzes their achievements and begins planning new initiatives, using the knowledge and experience gained.

Enhancing Innovative Approaches
Celebrating successes can stimulate innovation and a creative approach. Positive emotions and a sense of satisfaction can lead to a more open mindset toward new ideas and experimentation.

Example: An artist who receives recognition for their latest work is inspired to create new projects, using the support and positive feedback they have received.

Celebrating successes is crucial for maintaining motivation and achieving new goals. Creating positive associations, strengthening self-esteem, sustaining a positive cycle of motivation, and uncovering new opportunities make the celebration of achievements a powerful tool for ongoing growth and development. Remember to celebrate your successes and use them as a source of inspiration and energy for future accomplishments.

Methods of Celebrating Successes
Personal Celebration
Personal celebration can be simple yet effective. It may involve actions that bring you joy and satisfaction, such as buying something you've long wanted or spending time in a favorite place.

Example: After successfully completing a significant project, I decided to travel to a place I had always wanted to visit. This allowed me not only to relax but also to enjoy my achievement.

Celebrating with Others
Celebrating successes with family, friends, or colleagues can enhance positive emotions and make the process more meaningful. Joint celebrations help strengthen connections and create shared memories.

Example: After achieving a significant business goal, I hosted an evening with colleagues to celebrate our success. This allowed us not only to rejoice together but also to discuss the next steps.

Creating Traditions
Establishing your own traditions for celebrating achievements helps make the celebration process regular and systematic. This can be anything from a special dinner to annual events.

Example: I established a tradition of celebrating my achievements with a small dinner among close friends. This helps me not only to enjoy the outcome but also to maintain long-term motivation.

Using Success as Motivation
Reflecting on Achievements
Regularly reflecting on your successes helps you realize you can achieve your goals and overcome challenges. This reinforces self-confidence and motivates further action.

Example: I often review my list of achievements and recall moments when I overcame difficulties. This helps me see my progress and stay motivated.

Setting New Goals
Use your achievements as a platform for setting new goals and challenges. This will help you maintain constant growth and development.

Example: After completing a major project, I utilized the experience gained to set new goals and tasks. This allowed me not to rest on my laurels and strive for new heights.

Developing an Action Plan
Based on your accomplishments, develop an action plan for achieving new goals. Use your successes as a starting point for the next stage of development.

Example: After successfully launching a startup, I created a plan for developing a new product, leveraging the experience and knowledge gained from the previous project.

Success Stories
Examples of Notable Individuals
Studying the stories of successful people can inspire you and show how they used their achievements for further growth. This can help you apply their approaches to your own goals.

Example: J.K. Rowling, after publishing the first Harry Potter novel, not only celebrated her success but also used it to create subsequent books and expand her universe. This helped her continue her career and reach new heights.

Personal Examples
Personal examples and stories from your experience can also be inspiring. Share how celebrating your successes has helped you move forward and achieve new goals.

Example: Upon completion of my first major project, I felt more confident and motivated. This allowed me to take on new challenges and continue developing in my field.

Celebrating your successes is not only a way to enjoy what you have achieved but also an essential part of the motivation and personal growth process. Creating a systematic approach to celebrating achievements enables you to remember your efforts and results, which strengthens your motivation. When you recognize and celebrate your victories, you have the opportunity to pause and evaluate your journey, which enhances your self-confidence.

Using successes as motivation for new goals creates a positive cycle where each achievement inspires further efforts. This allows you not only to enjoy current results but also to prepare for new challenges and accomplishments. Constant attention to your successes fosters a positive attitude toward the goal attainment process, making it more engaging and fulfilling.

Studying the stories of successful individuals can also be a source of inspiration and support. Understanding how others have overcome difficulties and achieved success helps you see that your efforts are not in vain. Such examples remind us that success often comes after challenges and persistence.

Celebrating your victories, even the small ones, strengthens your self-confidence and fosters a positive attitude toward achieving goals. Each recognized achievement becomes a building block in your personal construction, forming a solid foundation for future successes. This process not only maintains a high energy level but also helps sustain motivation, ultimately contributing to your growth and prosperity in various areas of life.

Silencing the Inner Critic
Silencing the inner critic is an important step toward achieving your boldest goals. The inner critic often acts as an obstacle that hinders your actions, causing you to doubt your abilities and limiting your confidence. Sometimes its voice becomes so loud that you begin to believe in the negative beliefs it imposes.

To silence this inner voice, it is essential to recognize its influence on your thoughts and actions. Acknowledging that criticism may not be constructive but rather based on fears and doubts allows you to begin distancing yourself from it. Instead of accepting criticism as truth, try to replace negative thoughts with more positive and supportive ones.

Creating a habit of acknowledging your achievements and successes will also help shift the focus from criticism to recognizing your efforts. When you begin to celebrate your victories, even the small ones, it will strengthen your confidence and allow you to feel that you are capable of more. By learning the new habit of noticing positive moments, you can significantly change your internal dialogue.

Moreover, your environment plays an important role in silencing the inner critic. Interacting with supportive and inspiring people will help create a positive backdrop in which you can grow and develop. Instead of allowing criticism to suppress you, let those around you motivate and inspire you to achieve new heights.

By silencing your inner critic, you open the door to bold goals. This process requires time and effort, but it will become the foundation for your growth and success. You will be able to free yourself from limitations and allow yourself to dream and act without fear of failure. Ultimately, when you learn to silence that negative voice, you will have the opportunity to follow your aspirations and achieve significant heights you have always dreamed of.

The conclusion of this book summarizes how the energy of success can transform dreams into reality. By silencing your inner critic, you pave the way to achieve your boldest goals. This process requires awareness and willpower, but it leads to inner liberation and confidence in your abilities.

Understanding that you are capable of more will form the basis for actions that turn your ambitions into real achievements.

The energy of success comes from your intrinsic motivation and desire for self-improvement. It is not just a desire to achieve goals, but a deep understanding of your true desires and needs. When you silence your inner critic, you allow yourself to be vulnerable, opening up to new ideas and opportunities. This frees you from limiting beliefs that hinder your progress and creates space for growth and change.

Choosing supportive thoughts and environment also plays a crucial role on this journey. Engaging with people who inspire and support you helps strengthen your confidence and creates a positive backdrop on which your dreams can flourish. It's essential to surround yourself with those who believe in you and your potential, as this environment will promote your growth and support you during challenging times. Thus, forming a nurturing atmosphere around you becomes an integral part of the path to success.

By applying the methods and strategies described in this book, you can create a space where your dreams do not just remain dreams, but become the foundation for new accomplishments. Success is not just an end goal but a process where every victory and every overcoming is important. This journey requires persistence and patience, but every step you take brings you closer to your goals and opens new horizons.

Trust in your potential, open your heart to possibilities, and move forward with confidence. Your energy is the force that will guide you to new heights, making every achievement possible. Believe in yourself and your abilities, and the world will open up for you with new perspectives. Remember that success is not a final destination but a journey that requires you to be open to change and ready for new challenges.

By silencing your inner critic, you create a foundation for a successful life in which dreams become reality. You are capable of more than you think, and your pursuit of success is the key to your boldest goals. Allow yourself to dream, act, and achieve, and you will see how your energy transforms your life, filling it with meaning and accomplishments.

I CAN
I AM
I WILL
STRONG
I CAN
I AM
STRONG
I AM
STRONG
I AM
STRONG
I AM
I WILL
STROCIED
I AN
I WM
I WILL
SUCCEED

Chapter 19:
Long-Term Thinking: How to Stay One Step Ahead

This chapter discusses the importance of long-term thinking when it comes to achieving big goals. The author explains how forming a vision of the future helps make more informed decisions in the present and offers practical steps to develop the skill of long-term planning.

Often, people who focus on short-term results miss the opportunity to achieve something greater. It's essential to learn how to think ahead to not only achieve goals but also build lasting success. This chapter explores how thinking several steps ahead helps you stay on the right track, despite temporary challenges, and prepares you for unforeseen circumstances.

Defining Long-Term Thinking
What is long-term thinking?
Long-term thinking is the ability to see the bigger picture, plan for the future, and make decisions that will yield results years down the road. It's important not to limit yourself to short timeframes but to develop a strategy that leads to major life goals.

Examples of long-term thinking:
- A business owner who invests in team development, understanding that this will increase profits not immediately, but in a few years.
- An athlete who trains daily, knowing that the results will only show in the next season's competition.

Why Is Thinking Several Steps Ahead Important?

Preventing mistakes: Long-term thinking helps avoid impulsive decisions that may seem beneficial at the moment but lead to failure in the future.

Building sustainable success: Consistent actions aimed at long-term goals create a platform for stable and sustainable growth.

Forecasting risks and opportunities: Long-term thinking allows you to anticipate potential challenges and opportunities, giving you an advantage in preparing and managing them.

Developing Long-Term Planning Skills Setting goals for 5, 10, and 20 years ahead:
- How to formulate goals that cover extended timeframes.
- Tools for setting long-term goals: vision boards, 10-year plans, etc.

• The importance of adjusting goals at different stages of life.

Backward planning:
Define your ultimate goal and work backward step by step to understand what needs to be done at each stage.

Example: If your goal is to open a successful company in 10 years, think about what needs to be accomplished over the next 5 years, 2 years, and 6 months to achieve that.

Making Decisions with the Future in Mind
Mindfulness in decision-making:
How to make decisions that align with your long-term goals. For instance, temporarily increasing your workload may pay off significantly in the future.

Balancing short-term and long-term goals: It's not always possible to neglect current needs in favor of the future. Finding a balance between near-term achievements and those that require more time is essential.

Resource planning: How to allocate time, energy, and money with long-term prospects in mind.

Flexibility and Adaptation
Why flexibility is important:
Long-term thinking requires adaptability. Things don't always go as planned, so it's essential to be flexible and adjust to changes.

Revisiting goals: Regularly assess your progress and adjust your goals when necessary. This doesn't mean abandoning your dreams, but it allows you to take new opportunities and challenges into account.

Example: The story of someone who recalibrated their long-term goals based on experience and changing circumstances.

Tools for Developing Long-Term Thinking
Goal journaling: Regularly writing down goals helps track progress and adjust actions. Visualization techniques: Using visualization to strengthen your vision of long-term goals. This helps create a clear picture of the desired future and serves as a constant reminder of what you're striving toward. Mentors and advisors: How advice from experienced people who have already achieved success can help you craft a long-term strategy.

How Long-Term Thinking Improves Quality of Life

Confidence and calmness:
People who have a clear vision of their future experience less stress and greater confidence in their actions. They understand that their efforts lead to significant results, reducing the fear of failure.

Increased motivation:
When a person sees their ultimate goal and understands what their efforts are working toward, their motivation grows. Every step becomes part of a larger success.

Inspiring example:
The story of a well-known individual who achieved remarkable results thanks to long-term thinking.

Thinking one step ahead is a crucial skill that not only helps you achieve goals but also builds a sustainable and successful life. Long-term thinking allows you to maintain focus on what's important, make conscious decisions, and confidently move toward your dream. This chapter concludes the series of practical tools that will help you build your future on a solid foundation and turn your dreams into reality.

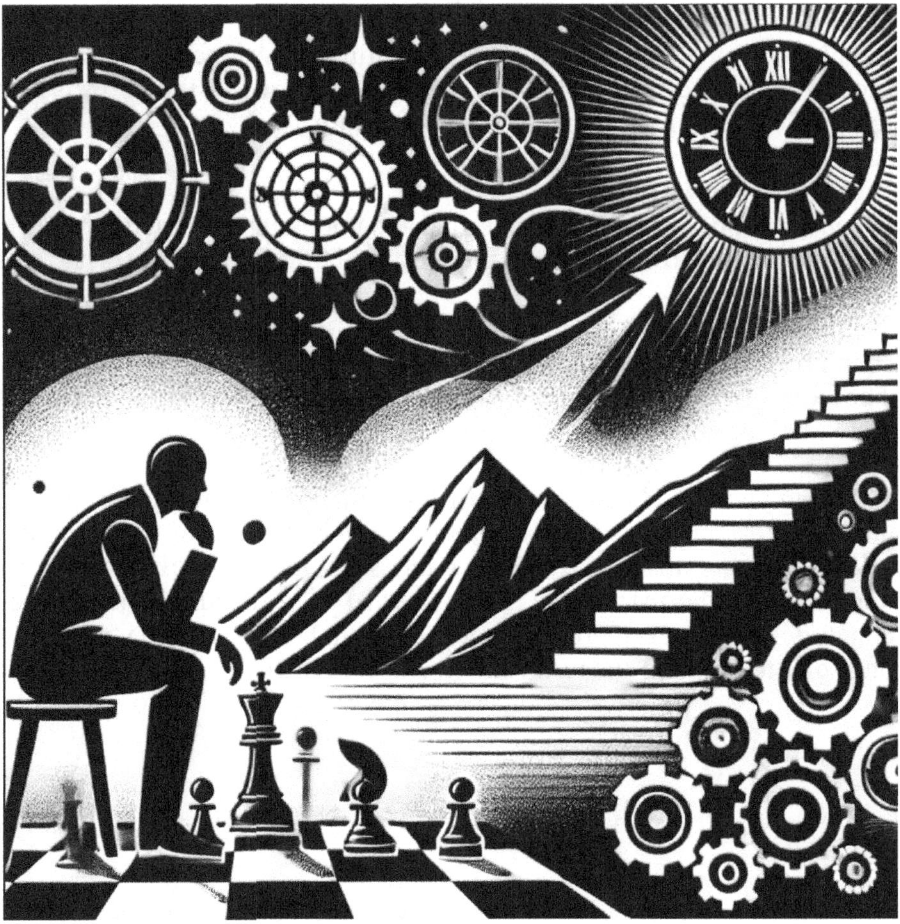

Chapter 20:
The Art of Networking

Networking is not just about exchanging business cards at an event or adding people to your social media. It's an active process of creating and maintaining mutually beneficial relationships that can play a crucial role in your success. In this chapter, we will explore how to develop networking skills and leverage them in your life to achieve your goals. Networking opens doors to new opportunities, resources, and support needed to fulfill your ambitions.

1. Understanding the Significance of Networking
Networking Connections as a Resource
Networking provides access to knowledge and resources that can be vital for your success. For instance, successful entrepreneurs often report that key moments in their careers are linked to important meetings and contacts. Connections can lead to new opportunities, business partnerships, and even investments. Many of us can recall instances where a chance meeting or conversation led to significant outcomes.

The Role of Recommendations
Recommendations from others can significantly boost your chances of success. In most cases, employers prefer to hire candidates they have heard positive feedback about. They trust the opinions of acquaintances and colleagues more than generic resumes. Building strong networking connections can help you receive recommendations that open doors you might never have dreamed of.

2. Strategies for Effective Networking
Defining Your Goals
Before embarking on active networking, it's essential to determine what you want to achieve. Do you want to find a new client, partner, or mentor? Having a clear understanding of your goals will help you focus on the right people and events. For example, if your goal is to find an investor, you should look for events where business people and investors are present.

Building Your Personal Brand
Your personal brand is how others perceive you. This is important because a strong personal brand can attract attention. To create a personal brand, start by analyzing your values and unique skills. Use social media to showcase your achievements and experiences. For instance, share articles you've written or projects you've worked on.

Active Participation in Events

Participating in professional events is one of the most effective ways to expand your network. Prepare in advance: research who will be speaking and what topics will be discussed. Don't hesitate to approach people and ask questions. For example, if someone shares an interesting experience, ask them for specific details.

3. Effective Communication Techniques
The Art of Conversation
Communication skills play a crucial role in networking. Start a conversation with a light greeting or compliment, then ask open-ended questions that require more detailed responses. Instead of asking, "How are you?" try "What's new in your business?" This will help create a deeper connection.

Paying Attention to Non-Verbal Cues
Non-verbal signals are a powerful tool in communication. Your posture, facial expressions, and even the pace of your speech can influence how you are perceived by others. Strive to be open and friendly: smile and maintain eye contact.

This creates a trusting atmosphere and helps you engage better with your conversation partner.

4. Developing Mutual Relationships
Maintaining Contact
Keeping in touch with people is an essential part of networking. Regularly check in to see how your contacts are doing and share interesting news. This could be a simple email or a message in a messenger app. It's important to show that you value the connection and are willing to maintain it.

Being Helpful
Remember that networking should be mutually beneficial. Look for opportunities to help others, whether it's providing information, introducing them to the right people, or assisting in solving their problems. This fosters an atmosphere of trust and respect, significantly strengthening your relationships.

5. Overcoming Barriers in Networking
Fear of Communication
Many people experience fear when it comes to meeting new individuals. You can overcome this fear through preparation and practice. For example, think ahead about what you want to say and rehearse your questions. Positive affirmations can also help boost your self-confidence.

Cultural Differences in Interaction
Be mindful of cultural differences that can affect your networking. Every culture has its norms of communication. For example, in some cultures, directness may be perceived as rudeness, while in others, it may be seen as a sign of honesty. Be attentive to the cultural context to avoid misunderstandings.

6. Leveraging Technology for Networking
Social Media
Platforms like LinkedIn can serve as powerful tools for creating and maintaining professional connections. Create a profile that reflects your experience and achievements. Don't hesitate to send friend requests to people you met at events and initiate conversations.

Virtual Events
With the rise of virtual events, participation has become more accessible. Join webinars and online conferences to meet people from anywhere in the world. Apply the same communication principles you would use at in-person meetings: ask questions and actively engage in discussions.

Conclusion
The art of networking is a powerful tool that can help you reach new heights in life and career. Building strong relationships based on trust and mutual assistance creates unique opportunities for growth and success. Remember that every meeting is an opportunity, and every interaction is a step toward achieving your dreams. Invest time and effort in developing your network, and you will see it bear fruit in the form of new opportunities and achievements.

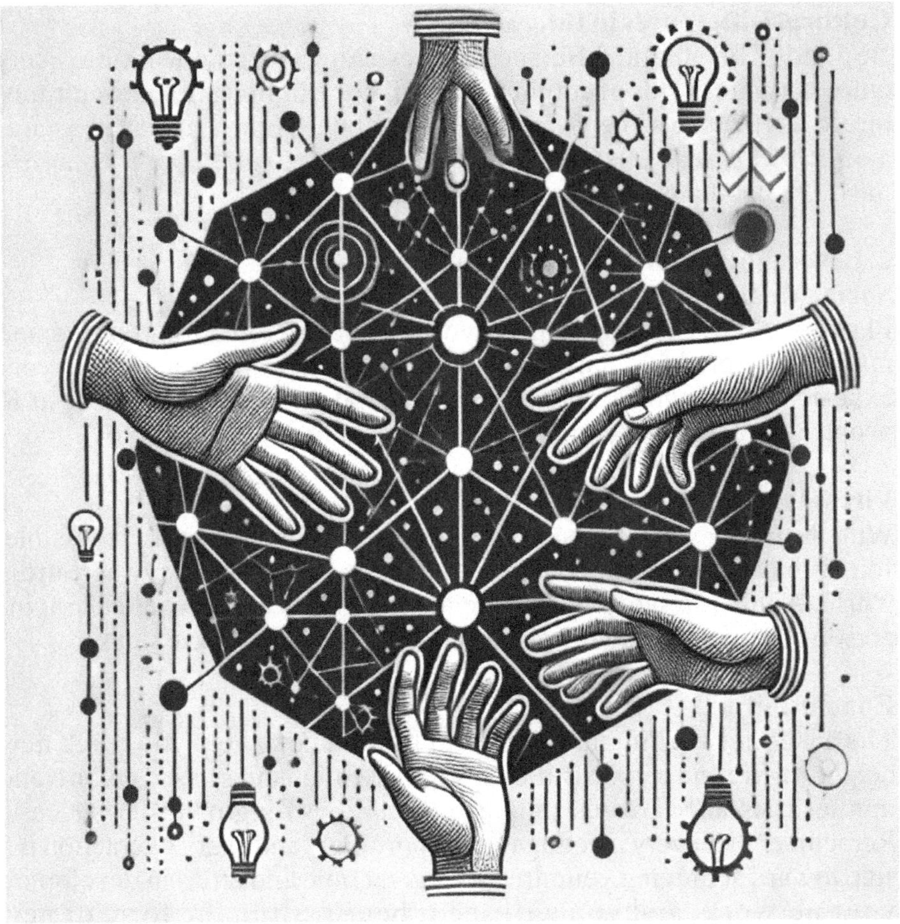

Chapter 21:
The Psychology of Success

The psychology of success is the study of how our thoughts, feelings, and behaviors influence our achievements and progress. This aspect of life is crucial to understanding why some people attain great success while others remain in the shadows of their potential. In this chapter, we will delve deeply into important psychological aspects such as positive thinking, self-confidence, and emotional management, and explore how these can be applied to achieve our goals.

1. Positive Thinking
Definition and Significance
Positive thinking is the ability to see opportunities even in challenging situations and to focus on solutions rather than problems. This approach does not mean ignoring difficulties; rather, it involves using them as a springboard for growth. Research shows that positive thinking can improve health, increase happiness levels, and lead to greater success.

Methods for Developing Positive Thinking
To cultivate positive thinking, start by analyzing your thoughts. Ask yourself questions like, "What can I learn from this situation?" or "How can this help me grow?" Keeping a journal of positive thoughts and achievements can also reinforce your positive outlook on life. Every evening, write down three positive events that occurred during the day and note your successes.

Impact on Achievements
Positive thinking helps you cope with setbacks, maintains motivation, and enhances resilience. When you approach life with optimism, you find it easier to overcome obstacles and failures. This, in turn, increases your chances of success in any endeavor.

2. Self-Confidence
What is Self-Confidence?
Self-confidence is the belief in your abilities and the assurance that you can achieve your goals. It is not only an internal feeling but also an external manifestation that influences how others perceive you. Confident individuals are more likely to take risks and embrace new challenges.

Factors Influencing Self-Confidence
Many factors affect confidence levels, including personal experiences, upbringing, and environment. For example, past successful experiences can bolster your confidence. Conversely, constant criticism or negative

comments can undermine your self-esteem.

Building Self-Confidence
To boost your confidence, start by setting small goals. Achieving them step by step will strengthen your belief in yourself. It's also important to work on your inner dialogue: replace negative thoughts with positive affirmations. Use affirmations—positive statements about yourself—to help shift your mindset.

3. Emotional Management
The Role of Emotions in Success
Emotions can significantly influence your behavior and decision-making. The ability to manage emotions is key to successful interactions with others and to self-regulation. For instance, learning to cope with anxiety and stress allows you to stay focused and make sound decisions.

Methods for Managing Emotions
Practicing mindfulness and meditation can help you better understand and control your emotions. Mindfulness is the state of being fully present in the moment, allowing you to recognize your feelings without judgment. Regular breathing exercises can also help calm you in stressful situations.

Emotional Intelligence
Emotional intelligence is the ability to recognize, understand, and manage your emotions and the emotions of others. It includes skills like self-awareness, self-regulation, empathy, and social skills. Developing emotional intelligence can help you communicate better and build relationships, which, in turn, contributes to success.

4. Motivation and Inner Drive
Types of Motivation
Motivation is divided into intrinsic and extrinsic types. Intrinsic motivation arises from within, when you act for your own goals and values. Extrinsic motivation, on the other hand, comes from external factors such as rewards and recognition. Both types of motivation are important, but intrinsic motivation often leads to more sustainable achievements.

Maintaining Motivation
To maintain your motivation level, set clear and achievable goals. It's also important to periodically review and update your goals to keep them relevant. Regular self-assessment helps you stay on track and make adjustments to your plans.

Creating Support
Building a supportive environment is another way to maintain motivation. Engage with people who share your goals and ambitions, and create a support network. This could be a group of like-minded individuals, a mentor, or simply friends who inspire you.

5. Overcoming Failures
Failure as Part of the Journey
Failures are inevitable on the path to success. It's important to view them as opportunities for learning and growth. Many successful individuals have faced numerous failures before achieving their goals. By analyzing your mistakes, you gain valuable insights that help you avoid them in the future.

Methods for Overcoming Failures
One way to cope with failures is to develop resilience. This means not allowing setbacks to stop you. Analyze your mistakes, learn from them, and move on. Regular mindfulness practice can also help you stay calm and composed during tough times.

6. Visualization of Success
What is Visualization?
Visualization is the process of creating vivid images of your goals and successes in your mind. This method helps you set your sights on achievements and strengthen your self-confidence. Many athletes and successful individuals use visualization to prepare for important events.

How to Practice Visualization
To effectively visualize your goals, find a quiet place, close your eyes, and picture yourself in a successful situation. Imagine how you achieve your goals and feel the emotions that fill you. Regular practice of visualization can help reinforce your belief in your abilities and enhance your motivation.

The psychology of success is a powerful tool that allows you to change your mindset and behavior to achieve greater heights. Positive thinking, self-confidence, emotional management, and motivation—all these aspects influence your path to success. Understanding and applying these concepts in everyday life can help you overcome obstacles and attain the desired outcomes. Start using these principles today, and you will notice how your life begins to improve for the better.

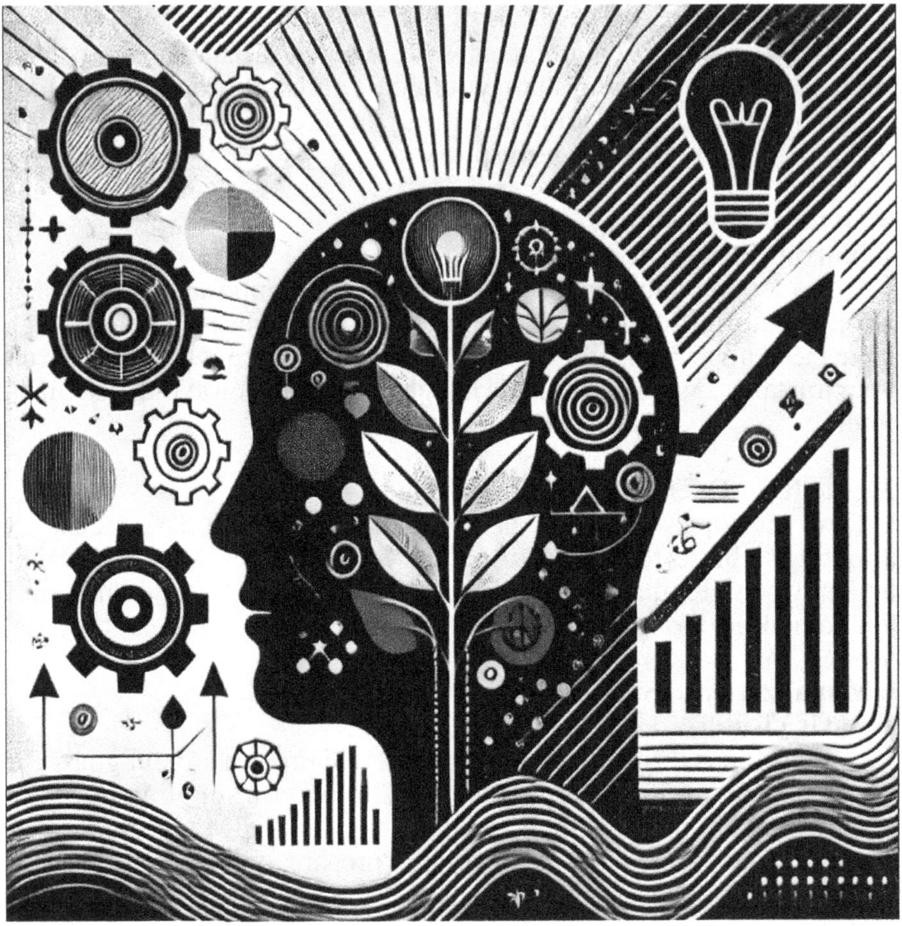

Chapter 22:
Conclusion: How the Energy of Success Turns Dreams into Reality

The final chapter of this book is dedicated to the art of completion and its significance in achieving goals. It's important to begin projects with enthusiasm but also finish them with a sense of fulfillment and awareness of what has been accomplished.

The Path to the Finish Line
When we set long-term goals, it often feels like the finish line is far away. In the beginning, there's a lot of excitement, but along the way, we face numerous challenges and struggles. However, what matters most is how we approach the final stages. Often, people abandon their important projects just when they are close to completion. This chapter delves into why finishing is so crucial and how to make it a part of your success strategy.

The Psychology of Completion
The feeling of completion:
Humans naturally seek to finish cycles. Unfinished tasks create feelings of anxiety and incompleteness. The psychological theory known as the "Zeigarnik Effect" suggests that unfinished tasks cause more mental tension than completed ones. The ability to finish projects brings satisfaction and allows you to move on to new goals without regret.

Why we fear finishing:
Sometimes, the fear of completion is rooted in the belief that success or failure will be final. Some people are afraid to acknowledge that the result might not meet their expectations, so they delay finishing. This chapter explains how to overcome this fear.

The Practice of Finishing
Setting final tasks: To successfully complete a project, it's important to break it down into small, manageable tasks that are easier to accomplish. A clear plan for the final steps helps you see the finishing process more clearly and ensures no important details are overlooked.

Setting deadlines: Even if a project extends over a long period, it's essential to establish a deadline for its completion. This adds structure to the process and prevents procrastination.

Letting go of perfectionism: Often, we don't finish things because we strive for perfection. But the reality is, perfection is unattainable. It's better to complete the work at a satisfactory level than to endlessly revise it and never finish.

Completion as a Skill
Developing the habit of finishing: Finishing is not just an action but a skill you can develop. Start with small tasks, complete them, and record these as successes. Gradually, move on to larger projects.

The principle of "one thing at a time": The ability to focus on one project and see it through to the end before starting something new allows you to manage your resources more effectively. Unfinished tasks can drain your energy, even if you never return to them.

Evaluating Results and Acknowledging Success
Assessing the work: After finishing, it's important not just to close the project and move on but also to take time to evaluate your progress. What did you do well? What could have been better? What lessons can you apply to future projects?

Celebrating success: Regardless of the outcome, it's important to celebrate the completion of a project. This could be something small, like a nice dinner or a day off, or something more significant, depending on the scale of the project. Celebration helps reinforce success in your subconscious and gives you the energy for new challenges.

Lessons from Finishing for the Future
Setting new goals based on completed ones: Completing one project gives you a powerful foundation for setting new, more ambitious goals. Evaluate what worked, and use this as a base for creating your next steps.

Strengthening the habit of completion: One completed project can become the foundation for a stronger habit of finishing what you start. Each new success strengthens your confidence and ability to see things through.

Stories of Completion
Real-life example: Including a story about a well-known person or company that successfully completed a major project despite difficulties will help readers understand that even successful people face challenges but know how to see things through to the end.

Personal example from the author: The author can share a personal story about how completing a difficult project led to new opportunities and further growth.

Mistakes to Avoid When Finishing
Dragging out the process: One of the most common enemies of finishing is dragging out the final steps. The longer you postpone the final actions, the harder it becomes to complete what you've started.

Lack of a clear endpoint: Some projects can drag on indefinitely if you don't establish clear criteria for completion. It's important to define what "finished" means to avoid being stuck in endless revisions.

Forgetting to celebrate: Sometimes, people get so consumed by the process that they forget to celebrate their achievements. Don't let yourself skip this important stage—rewarding yourself for your hard work helps recharge your energy for future goals.

Finishing as the Start of a New Journey
Completion is not the end, but the beginning of a new path. When you finish one project, new opportunities and perspectives open up. The key is to learn how to finish satisfactorily and use that experience for the future. Completion is the key to confidence, self-discipline, and continual growth, This conclusion summarizes everything covered in the book and helps the reader understand that the energy of success is not just about achieving specific goals, but about a deeper process of internal transformation. Success is not a final destination, but a state which you move through life, constantly evolving, overcoming challenges, and reaching new heights. The main idea is that the energy of success flows through all aspects of your life—from your thoughts and beliefs to your actions and results.

The entire book was built around the concept of the energy of success—the force that helps individuals turn dreams into reality. The conclusion deepens this concept. The energy of success is not just motivation and the drive toward goals but also your ability to manage your emotions, inner resources, and environment. This energy requires constant nourishment through awareness of your values, development of inner strength, and the ability to adapt to changes.

Imagine your success as a river. When you channel your efforts correctly and surround yourself with positive people, the water flows smoothly and quickly. But when obstacles such as fear, doubt, or a negative environment appear, the river may slow or stop. Your job is to continually clear the path of your river, removing obstacles and guiding the flow of energy in the right direction.

One of the central ideas of the book is that success is a process, not a final point. Finishing one project or achieving one goal is not the end—it is merely a step toward something greater. It's important not just to achieve goals but to enjoy the process of reaching them. The conclusion emphasizes that every success is a stepping stone to new horizons.

A person who achieves one significant goal, such as starting a business, doesn't stop there. They learn, grow, implement new ideas, and set even more ambitious goals. This constant process of growth is the foundation of success.

The energy of success is directly connected to your personal development. The more you grow as an individual, the stronger your energy becomes, and the greater your chances of achieving success. The conclusion emphasizes that success is inseparably linked with self-awareness and continuous work on yourself. If you want your dreams to become reality, you need not only to set goals but also to develop the qualities necessary for achieving them: persistence, patience, courage, and the willingness to learn from mistakes.

An athlete preparing for the Olympics doesn't just train physically. They work on mental resilience, learn to deal with failures, develop confidence, and focus on long-term goals. This is the same approach you must apply in any area of life if you want to achieve outstanding results.

In the process of achieving success, it's important to learn how to silence the inner critic that prevents you from moving forward. The conclusion highlights that the inner voice of doubt and fear is often the biggest obstacle to reaching your goals. However, by learning to recognize this voice and replace it with positive thoughts and affirmations, you free yourself from unnecessary limitations. You learn to trust your potential and embrace failure as part of the journey to success.

For example, a writer who has put off writing their book for years due to fear of criticism finally realizes that their inner voice was based on false beliefs. They decide to start writing despite potential mistakes, and in the end, they publish their book.

This is how the energy of success turns dreams into reality, which gains recognition. This example demonstrates that silencing the inner critic is a key step toward transformation and success.

Another important aspect of the energy of success is the ability to find sources of motivation and inspiration. The conclusion explores various ways to maintain a high level of motivation, even when circumstances are not in your favor. It is essential to surround yourself with people who support you and engage in activities that bring you joy and inspiration.

In closing, it is important to emphasize that success is not a static point but a continuous journey forward. Even when one goal is achieved, there are always new horizons ahead. The conclusion wraps up with the idea that true success is not found in specific results but in the process of continuous growth, self-improvement, and the willingness to move forward despite challenges.

The energy of success is your personal source of strength that will accompany you throughout your life. Every new step, every goal achieved brings you closer to realizing your boldest dreams and opens up new perspectives.

Made in the USA
Coppell, TX
03 March 2025

46622622R00085